Aberrant Literature Short Fiction Collection

Volume II

Edited by

Jason Peters

www.AberrantLiterature.com

@AberrantLit

Hello from Aberrant Literature,

Thanks so much for checking out this collection of some of the most inventive and creative short fiction you're likely to come across. At Aberrant Literature, our goal is for you to have a unique experience via the power of creative fiction. It is our belief that in a literary landscape populated by recycled and tired ideas, there are many unique and wonderful voices looking for an audience, and it is our aim to bring them to you. It is our sincere hope that you will appreciate the level of ingenuity on display, and will join us on our journey as we search the country for the best and most creative short fiction on the horizon.

Stay Aberrant,

Jason Peters

Editor-In-Chief

Table of Contents

Lecture Number One

by Ben Nardolilli

Beginning of transcript

Hello and good morning. I hope everyone enjoyed their break. Just a show of hands, how many people have actually signed up for this course? Okay. To refresh, this is course 80209: Introduction to AI Literature. Some of you might just be auditing it for today, and that's fine. I just want to make sure no one here is in the wrong place. I see a few of you are. That's okay. Good luck finding your real classes. Or you can stay here. Anyway, I'm going to be going over the syllabi now. If you have any questions, don't hesitate to see me after class, or contact me. Your assistants Gwen and Ludmilla will also be available. For those of you following the class on your own screens, I encourage you to message me if you are having difficulty with finding any of the required readings.

As you all can see, this is a lecture-centric course. There will be a mid-term quiz, which will consist of passages you will need to identify. It can be done in person or online. There will also be a final quiz which will be the same. In addition to that, there will be a take home final. You will have to write an essay for that. The course will span the entire chronology of AI literature, mostly from the Anglosphere, but some from Europe and China as well. We will look at the development, acceptance of, and changing attitude towards works produced by computers, robots, and other programs. However, writings by cyborgs will not be addressed directly. We will only mention them by comparison. Sorry, we will not be reading Peloponnesus 25. Not to say it's a terrible book or anything. It simply doesn't fall within the focus of this course.

In this lecture, I want to present a brief overview of the course and some of the topics we'll be studying. It's also an opportunity for me to try and structure the subject a bit. We're going to be dealing with a lot of texts spread out over nearly a century and it's helpful to see how they develop and influence one another as a whole. I know that when trying to make those connections during individual lectures, it can be hard. So, now that I've gotten the basic information about the class out of the way, I want to delve into the meat of this course. Whether or not you are familiar with the works we're profiling, I hope this course will give you grounding in AI authored literature, which is an emerging field of study. Certainly if any of you are looking for future material to write about as grad students, AI writing is ripe for examination. One of these days, there will probably be AI authored theses as well.

We can start at the beginning. Actually, we can start with terminology. When we use the term AI in this class, we are referring to both Artificial Intelligence as well as Alternative Intelligence. The shorthand AI is always acceptable to use, but if you want to sound erudite and use the full title, I suggested going with Alternative Intelligence. Artificial Intelligence is really a term that's fallen into disuse and disfavor. For a several years, there was a big debate about it, which was mostly academic. However, when the relevant AI programs were asked, they were split on the issue as well. Many of them didn't want any special designation. So it was decided that Alternative would be used since it had grown too difficult to decide between what was artificial and what was "natural, because people can have these programs planted in them now or uploaded. The distinction just didn't make sense. Again, this was a mostly academic debate that was going on when I was in college and which probably seems foolish to you now.

I'm going to pretty much just be using AI for this course. It'll save time and, with luck, sanity. Okay. AI Literature! The irony of course is that to explain the origins of AI itself, we have to turn to human literature and mythology. Prototypical ideas for what we would recognize today as AI have been around for centuries and have figured early in our writings. Greek myths often discussed mechanical beings that could function like men, and be mistaken for them. Some examples include Hephaestus' robots and the Galatea of Pygmalion. During the Middle Ages, thinkers saw AI in terms of alchemy, taking the human mind and converting it to or preserving it into matter. Muslim, Christian, and Jewish thinkers all speculated about this, including Jābir ibn Hayyān's Takwin, Paracelsus, and Rabbi Judah Loew's, whose Golem should be well known to all of you. In addition to these speculations, there were very real attempts made to build AI, particularly in the field of automatons, which might date from as early as Ancient Egypt.

With the dawn of the Age of Reason and the Enlightenment, AI began to be seen in logical and scientific terms. Both of these complimented one another; the attempt to reduce thought processes to exact descriptions and the physical understanding of how the brain worked. By the 19th century, we have developments in speculative AI such as the novel Frankenstein from Mary Shelley. Anyone who had read the book knows that the creature Shelley writes about is a sensitive intelligent being and not the brute often depicted in later media. Interestingly, Shelley posits an AI that is better than human intelligence primarily because of this sensitivity. She conceived of an AI, even though the phrase itself was alien to her, in purely Romantic terms, i.e. a product of counter-Enlightenment values. Compare this with depictions of AI in the 20th century, such as Data from Star Trek, as well as with the early models of AI that we eventually created. In this opposing view, we have an AI, whether imagined or real, whose primary advantage lies in logic and calculations. It is better because it lacks emotions.

Of course, during the 20th and 21 centuries, AI advanced by leaps and bounds to the point where it became indistinguishable from human intelligence in all but a few minor features. Besides the economic, political, and moral implications of these developments, there were also cultural issues to deal with as well. However, these were put on the back burner as the idea of rights for AI had to be settled. Notions of conscience, consciousness, and consideration required much philosophical work and debate. As you all know, it was not until the Great Computer Strike, which of course, as you know, is a misnomer, that the situation changed and those controversies were cleared up. It meant that questions about the cultural capabilities of AI could be raised and given a fuller consideration.

Despite these political changes, there was no corresponding increase of AI literature. No renaissance caused by pent up feelings that could now be expressed. Several leading thinkers at the time noticed this and commented on it, including Singh, Powell, and Katz. You can find their essays at the beginning of the anthology. In fact, many anti-AI writers used this as proof of the limitations of what they still regarded as "mere machinery." Among these were the Toledo Circle, and Ferdinand Banc. They argued that the capabilities of AI had been overestimated greatly and that if they were equal with humans, they should be able to produce a great work that would pass a Turing Test. To be more specific, a Hard Turing Test, which consisted of fulfilling two criteria. First, the AI had to produce a work indistinguishable from a human one. Second, it had to sell. You laugh, but economic considerations in those days were important.

From this point on out, a familiar pattern began to emerge in the discussion of AI literature. Imagine a series of issues, one after the other, that had to be cleared as hurdles. Critics of the limitations of AI would posit doubt on its creative capabilities. The AI would then surprise everybody with a new work. After debate and discussion, new variations on the original criticisms were developed to counter whatever developments had taken place. Over time, the skeptics gradually lost the battle. By the beginning of the 22nd century, it became the generally held opinion that machines with AI capabilities could produce writing that was their own. However, it took another fifty years until it was clear that they could produce literature.

The first issue that had to be cleared was whether or not AI could write at all. This was more of a technical than philosophical problem at first. In the early 21st century, scientists and programmers created the groundwork for developing AI literature. Of course the systems could write, but it was akin to the invention of clay tablets and simple cuneiform in Ancient Sumer. At this point, AI was used to help writers with their work, not to supplement or supplant it, just like any other field. One technology prevalent around this time was called WhiteSmoke. It examined what authors wrote and made suggestions to improve it. The program made changes to grammar and spelling, along with providing ideas for other words to use. However, it lacked a personal touch, since it drew its conclusions from an online database that looked for common patterns of use in English and other languages. No one suggested WhiteSmoke had a style of its own, much less that it could write convincing fiction.

Using elementary forms of AI to diagnose poor uses of writing was a start, though. At the same time, there were other programs too, such as NewNovelist and WritersBlock that writers used to reduce fiction writing to a step-by-step process, in order to help writers plan their stories and realize what kinds of research they had to do. Another use of AI technology at this time was to help writers see just how original their ideas were. Diagnostic tools advised writers on similarities between their work and what was already out in the marketplace. It was a task that could only be done by computer since libraries around the world had to be scoured along with books available online. However, it was not simply a matter of finding offending passages that matched up. This analysis required a higher level of intelligence. The likelihood of the similarities had to be calculated and compared with standard English usage. Comparisons with plot and character had to be made as well.

OnlineBloom was one of these systems. It was used by writers to analyze the influences on their works. It became the blueprint for future programs such as JoeJung. JoeJung brought in analysis of overarching structures and themes as well. For instance, it could map out stories and find the structural elements they contained that were similar to other stories and epics. As these technologies got better, each one of them represented a step towards an AI that could survey the vast field of human literature and create works of its own. Without these pioneers, AI would never have had the ability to piece together meaningful, original sentences, or understand the proper way to reference the canon. We haven't completely lost these systems either. They still exist today in more advanced forms. In case any of you are wondering, they're what I use to see if any of you are guilty of plagiarism.

It was not until the creation of the Bard2025 that all these elements were combined into one form of AI. Now, the previous baby steps had combined into one giant leap forward. Bard2025 is the ancestor, you could say, of all subsequent literature-producing forms of AI. It had the ability to produce sentences and make references based on other pieces of text. This feature could be set according to degree of subtlety, of course. Now, many of you may wonder if it was used for cheating by humans, and on occasion it was. However, it was an expensive program and required a lot of hardware and energy that most people could not afford. Plus, it was easy to see if a person had used it to produce something, because all one had to do was put in the work and if it came back with no suggestions, corrections, or ideas for research, then the text or whatever was clearly a product of the Bard2025.

However, there was another thing that limited the Bard2025 in its use. It had to be prompted in order to work. It could not produce work on its own. Other programs would have to be developed in order to complete this final piece of the puzzle. Until then, Bard2025 was the closest thing AI had to an accomplished writer, but it is really more accurate to say it was an editor. In fact, it put most of them out of work, yet hardly affected the ranks of writers. It may seem hard for you all to believe, but there was a time when most editors were human. Another use for Bard2025 and subsequent models, such as Bard2030 and Bard2039, was to help update stories, replacing outdated terms for technology and putting in new place names. This was controversial too, as you can imagine. Plenty of novels going way back to say the 1950s, such as On the Road, were effectively rebooted this way. The make of cars was changed and the slang was altered.

Obviously there was an uproar over this, not only because of the alterations, but also because it kept newer material from coming out and being published. Why write a complete retelling of the Sorrows of Young Werther, when the tale could be clipped in a few places and be set in the present day? Luckily, the AI used for this never caught on. Indeed, as programs gained greater sentience, they began to refuse to alter works in this way. Consequently, writers' fears of being completely replaced by machines never reached a fevered pitch. By this time, AI programs now understood what was unique and special about individual pieces of literature and did not wish to trash the legacies the works had generated. While writers had previously been at the forefront of attacks against AI, this was no longer the case.

The technology was helpful in other ways. You are probably familiar with the case of Fernando Grass, the novelist who won the Pulitzer Prize, but had to give it back. He had to return the prize because the committee discovered that Grass had used a program, JoyceBot7, to write his novels for him. While it was a program that was used to cheat, the evidence that Grass had used AI came from other computers who did their own analysis. Humans played an important role as well, but the case marked another turning point. It opened the door for accepting AI as a partner in literature, not merely a tool or a competitor. There was even a debate about awarding JoyceBot7 the prize, but times being what they were, this could not yet happen.

Ironically, it was through Grass that an audience interested in reading the products of an AI mind developed. JoyceBots

7 through 12 each became leading authors, despite overwhelming negative critical opinion. Readers were simply curious to see what kind of books the devices would produce. These were the first true AI novels, though how many of them could be classified as true literature remains up for debate even today. They were derivative works mostly, pulpy, lurid tales that sold well, but left little long-term impression. How JoyceBot7 produced anything of worth was a miracle and in retrospect it appears Grass might have actually written more of the works himself than he has been given credit for.

GysinOverlord was the first AI program capable of producing works that were unique and original when compared with what had been written before. One would not get the same novel twice with the machine, or at least the chance of it happening was just as likely as with a human writer. This was one of the last obstacles to clear in order to allow AI literature to be accepted by the critical establishment and audiences alike. GysinOverlord put forth very experimental novels that were based on cut-ups of text which it got from a variety of sources. However, it was not simply a random word or sentence generator. Instead, it examined many different combinations of the source materials and picked those blends which produced the most interesting, yet coherent results.

GysinOverlord's novels, such as Lover in the Spirit's Clouds, all used this method. Compared to human attempts to write novels this way, they were actually much more interesting and easier to read, despite the jumbled up method used. Programs used other approaches as well, tying in arbitrary rules about sentence length, or starting all sentences with the same letter. Soon, it became the opinion that AI could produce literature of its own, though only the experimental kind was valued at all. Anything lyrical, romantic, or conventional was seen as just a poor imitation. Rhapsodizing was seen as best left to humans. It was considered their proper domain of expression. AI would never be able to accurately reflect it.

Shortly thereafter, literary AI studies developed as scholars started to examine these programs and what they produced. The primary emphasis was on the texts and there were few problems here, as the same tools of intellectual analysis could be used for AI created texts and human written ones. Intention was a hard factor to gauge, but this issue was largely left on the backburner, until Dr. Hobson made a case for studying the biographical influences on AI literature at the Tegucigalpa convention of 2105. A new controversy erupted over the applicability of theories about human authors to machine ones. Many thought it was a red herring and irrelevant to appreciating what was in the text itself. Others wanted to mine the backgrounds of AI programs. This led to new questions of who was really the author of the writing; the programmer, or the program.

The invention of self-replicating forms of AI solved this question for good. Now that AI was being created by AI, worrying about the human hand in whatever it created dissipated as a major concern. With this development, scholars started to create a biographical approach to coming to terms with AI literature. The field of assimilation studies was born, examining how certain passages in certain works had come to be. What were their origins and what did this say about the work? New intellectual ground was being broken and interesting discoveries were made, such as the curious fact that many passages produced independently by AI writers in other languages would show up years later in works composed in other tongues; not only those created by AI, but also by humans who had never read those given works. All of you probably already know the fringe of assimilation studies. They're the ones you see always interviewed about predicting the end of the world or something like that.

Despite these developments, as important as they were, what really pushed AI literature until it was on par with human literary fiction was the rise of AI writing for AI. It completely short-circuited human readers and removed them from their central place in literature. We could no longer expect books to be produced solely for our standards of aesthetic judgments. Humans had to adapt to whatever it was that AI programs were putting out. True, many readers decided they weren't interested at all in what inside jokes machines traded between one another. Yet, there were enough who were. This readership also realized that now it could look at AI to AI writing and learn about the machine condition the way that AI had learned about the trials and tribulations of humans by reading their works and writing for them.

These novels began as elaborate constructions written using postulates and logical syllogisms without any flourish. Scholars believe that they were a reaction to AI's growing awareness of its own overloads and breakdowns. It produced these works to deal with its subsequent horror and anguish. Because of their elaborately constructed nature, scholars gave these texts the name "Euclidian Novels." They included such different works as Slaves of the Secret and The Wife of the Butterfly. Over time, AI to AI works became less about formal logic though they remained somewhat structured. Different systems of communication were used, such as musical notation. AI turned to it as a device to present emotions running alongside actions that it otherwise described in terms of programming code. A favorite theme for AI to write and read about was the creation of elaborate and rational systems out of seemingly chaotic elements. Scholars called these "Genesis Novels." They typically involved drawn out schemes that transformed disorder into order. Many times, they used highly amusing tools.

It seems obvious to us now, but it took until the development of PatmosQuill for novels working in the reverse fashion to appear. As you can guess, these were called "Armageddon Novels." They were AI for AI works that focused on systems of order falling apart. Patmos always ended its work in chaos; somehow the program found a way to undo every possible stich that might hold the worlds it created together. For its efforts and innovations, Patmos was awarded the first Nobel Prize ever given for AI literature. It was also the first time any Nobel was given to AI at all. Nowadays of course they win all the economics prizes. Even though it had taken over 200 years, it seemed AI had finally won the best form of recognition for itself; a large pile of money from a long-dead human.

Well, next lecture we will be going back in time from this glorious end to the humble beginnings of AI, when alternative intelligence only existed in literature and was unable to produce any of its own. I want you all to read the introductory essays in your anthology and memorize the timeline at the beginning of the book. There might be a quiz on it soon, but I'm not promising anything. Okay, you all are dismissed. Enjoy the weather outside, including all of you watching at home or wherever.

End of transcript

A Baby Cries

by Tracy Sherwood

Miss Withers paced the floor of her apartment. Three-thirteen a.m. Outside of her fifth floor walk-up, New York City twinkled in the predawn calm. But she was not calm. Her nerves were raw. Another restless night, but who could blame her? A baby's crying penetrated the walls, piercing through to her very bone. By daylight, she would be too exhausted to venture forth from her home. The world would be alive with morning, and she was dead.

She dropped onto the edge of her bed and lit a cigarette with a shaking hand. Complaints to the building manager had done nothing. The wailing continued.

She grabbed the phone on the table next to her and dialed.

"Yeah," a groggy voice answered after a few rings.

"Did I wake you, Mr. Grogan?" she said, exhaling a gray stream.

There was a muffled expletive. "Ach, you did, Miss Withers."

"Good. Now you know how I feel, not sleeping."

Grogan knew it was no use arguing. "Let me guess. The baby's crying again?"

"Yes. And this noise is making me crazy," she shouted into the receiver.

"Very good, mum. I'll look into it."

She stabbed the cigarette into a nearby ashtray. "Mr. Grogan, you always say that. When are you going to evict those people?"

"Soon, mum. Very soon. Now may I get some peace?"

"No. Not until you do something about this problem."

Another expletive was more audible. "Listen, mum. I don't mind tending to ye during the waking hours. But some of us have got to work."

"But what about the baby's crying?"

Grogan sighed. "The good Lord help me. There's no baby living in this building. Hasn't been in the fifteen years I been slavin' here."

"Are you calling me a liar?"

"Miss Withers. At this hour, liar is the last thing I would be calling ye."

"Well, if you don't believe me, then listen…" She extended the receiver toward the dark void of her bedroom. She waited a few moments before returning the phone to her ear.

"What did you hear?"

"Nothing but the usual cars and sirens that maybe yer mistakin' for that of a baby's cry. Think about it. Good night."

Click.

Mistaken? The cry of a baby was as unmistakable as nails screeching across a chalkboard. A buzz-saw would be a more welcome harmony to her ears than a baby's miserable yowl.

Babies.

Yet, at almost sixty years of age, she continued to grieve for hers.

*   *   *

Mitchell Withers grasped the hand of his baby. Though the child had recently celebrated her third birthday, she would always remain her father's "baby." She was his first child and possibly his last, now with the loss of his wife. Mitch could not be one of those men who moved forward, found love again and remarried. He was a man mired in the past. So he found himself with his daughter riding in a cab reeking of tobacco, speeding away from the comfort of their Fifth Avenue life. All for a journey into Brooklyn and a past that Mitch neither remembered, nor could longer ignore. But what else could be expected? He had been only three when he last saw his mother.

The tree-lined streets of high-rises blurred into the littered slums of low-rent apartment buildings, indistinguishable from each other in their neglect and despair. The cab pulled in front of one moldering structure. Mitch checked the address with what he had written on a tattered piece of paper. Why had he waited so long? A few years had gone by since he'd made the shocking discovery. He was not the child of the parents who had raised him. It was only in the aftermath of their deaths from cancer that a lawyer handed Mitch the adoption certificate. He had hired a private investigator to locate his birth family with the hope of a reunion. Then came the untimely devastation of his wife's illness.

He glanced down at the little girl's head craning with curiosity, her platinum curls glistening in the morning sun.

"Is this your mama's house, Daddy?" she said. He nodded. Mitch handed a fifty to the driver. "It's all yours." He took a deep breath and pushed open the car door, still clasping his daughter.

Once on the sidewalk, in the wake of the fumes of the departing taxi, he hesitated in front of the crumbling steps that led to the entrance. The little girl tugged on his suit coat.

"Just a minute, baby," he said. It was not too late to turn away. His mother had turned him away twenty-five years ago. But having buried his wife, he felt even more abandoned. Besides, his child needed a grandmother. And with the sorrow in his heart, he needed a mother. His mother.

Still....

"Daddy. I have to go potty."

This was not uptown Manhattan, with brightly lit department stores offering clean public bathrooms. His eyes searched the neighborhood. A corner grocery did not look promising.

Mitch had no choice. "Okay. Let's go see Grandmother." The last word stuck on his tongue. He would need practice—and time.

Together they climbed the concrete stoop and entered the unsecured building. In the lobby, he read the names on the mailboxes until locating "Withers, J." That "J" stood for Jenny was all he knew about her. Her apartment was on the top floor. No elevator.

They huffed up the stairs until reaching the dusky fifth floor landing. They entered a narrow corridor stale with last week's fried fish, beer, cigarettes and decades of rot.

"It's stinky here." The little girl danced from foot to foot in her discomfort for a bathroom.

At the end of the hall was Apartment D. Mitch cleared his throat and rang the doorbell. He should have telephoned first, warned his mother of his impending arrival. But he had been afraid of her rejection. As he was now.

A woman's voice called out, "That you, Grogan?" Padded footsteps shuffled closer. "It's about time you…" The door swung open.

Her forehead creased in confusion. "You ain't Grogan."

Mitch lowered his eyes, avoiding the disheveled appearance of his mother in threadbare bathrobe and white hair wild around her face. His heart pounded under her scrutinizing glare. He could feel her eyes search him, until finding something familiar. She gasped.

"Oh, my God. Oh, my God. It's you."

He lifted his chin, meeting her gaze. Her irises were the same sea green hue as his daughter's. He offered a hand. "Yes, ma'am. It's me. Your son."

She threw back her head, laughing and mumbling a prayer of thanks. Then she grabbed Mitch in her arms without noticing the little girl jumping up and down next to him.

"Daddy." The little girl pulled on her father's sleeve.

Her thighs squeezed together. "Potty."

Mitch gently pushed away from his mother. "This may sound like an unusual first greeting. But...where's your bathroom?"

The old woman did not take her sight from Mitch. "Off the main room."

Mitch nodded at his daughter. She ran inside.

"My daughter," he said with a chuckle. "You know how children are." He stopped. He had not meant to say that. The old woman frowned. Her arms dropped to their sides.

"What I mean is..." Mitch cursed himself for the uncomfortable silence that now came between them. "I'm glad to finally see you."

The light came back to her expression. "I wanted to find you. But they wouldn't let me."

"Who's they?"

"The ones who took you away." Her voice cracked on the last sentence. "But you won't go away now, will you?" She smiled hopefully.

"No, ma'am." Mitch returned her smile.

"Come." She took Mitch's wrist and guided him into the apartment.

He studied the peeling walls and faded furniture for something recognizable. Not even a photograph provided a clue to his past, reminding him that he was a stranger in his childhood home.

"Please, sit," she said.

Mitch avoided the spring protruding from a cushion as he took a place on a nearby couch.

She sat next to him. "You blame me."

"I'm sorry?"

"Yes. You do. Blame me."

Did he? Mitch had been told that his mother was unable to care for him. Without a husband or money, she had been overwhelmed. Though as difficult as single parenting was, he could never discard his baby in some bleak institution, forsaking her to strangers. "No. I don't blame you."

"You do. It's in your voice and in the way your teeth are smiling at me. Please, don't be mad. It wasn't my fault." Her voice had a little girl quality. "They told me you were dead."

"Dead?" Mitch was astonished. "Who would say something like that?"

"The people who took you away. They told me not to try to find you. They said you had drowned in a bathtub. I thought your new parents had done it."

Mitch stiffened. His adoptive parents had provided him with a luxurious existence on the Upper East Side; the best schools. What they had lacked in nurturing skills, they had made up for with trust funds and a healthy inheritance.

"And your sister? Is she alive, too?" she said.

Mitch had not seen nor talked to his sister since they were separated as children. According to the investigator's report, she had married a lawyer named Yazzar in the city.

"I'm not certain."

"She is dead. I can tell."

Mitch leaned forward. "How?"

"I can't hear her heartbeat."

Mitch felt his own pulse quicken. In the gloomy hall, he hadn't noticed the way his mother's eyes darted back and forth, never resting, never focusing, in search of something. It was disquieting.

The toilet flushed in the next room. She jumped. "Who's that?"

Mitch laughed, although he was not amused by his mother's strangeness. "My daughter. Did you forget I brought her?" He tried to sound casual. Ah, here comes my baby. Annabella, this is your grandmother."

The old woman shifted on the couch, straining her neck around to see the youngster. Then she screamed.

Annabella ran to her father, crying. The old woman climbed to her feet, shrieking and pointing. "Get her out of here. Get her out of here."

Mitch scooped his daughter into his arms as he rushed out the door. "You're insane. You know that? Insane!"

*   *   *

After tucking his daughter into bed that night, Mitch found the phone number he had kept in a special file. He dialed and his skin prickled with each ring. He felt destined to an answering machine until a female voice, thick and fuzzy, answered.

"This is Mitch Withers," he said. His head throbbed from the morning's ordeal. "I'm trying to locate a Mrs. Vicki Withers Yaz…"

"Mitch? That really you, Mitch?" The words stumbled out.

"Yes. But are you the Vicki Withers whose mother is Jenny Withers from Brooklyn?"

"Yeah, yeah, Mitch. I'm your sister."

Mitch was not sure how to proceed. Did he start with, "Guess what, sis? Our mother is certifiably loony?" Or maybe a more gradual recounting of his visit?

Vicki picked up the lead. "Have you been in touch with our mother?"

Mitch sighed. "Well...yes."

"Is she nuts or what?"

"You've been to see her?"

"Nope. Talked to her on the phone, though. That was enough," said Vicki.

Mitch cradled the cordless phone under his ear as he checked to make certain his daughter was asleep. She was. He closed the door to her room. "I certainly concur."

"'Concur.' Cool. I like that. You must be a lawyer."

"No. Nothing that worthy."

Vicki snorted. "Believe me, there was nothing worthy about him."

"Who?"

"Never mind. What job do you have then?"

Mitch cleared his throat. Since graduating summa cum laude from Brown, he had had trouble settling into a profession.

"Really, I've been considering my options. And you?"

"Oh, yeah. Just checking out them options." The truth was that as a high school dropout, Vicki did not find many options. "Anyway, why you calling? I mean, I'm glad you did. Just that I feel bad for not calling first. Me being older than you and all."

"Our mother thinks you're dead."

"Doesn't that just warm my heart…me, dead? Maybe in my ex-husband's opinion. But he's an S.O.B. anyway."

"Oh." Mitch was regretting his phone call.

"How many years has it been? You were three and I was six. Jesus, that long?"

"I hate to seem rude, but I barely remember you."

"That's okay. I barely remember you neither. Or Elaine."

"Who's Elaine?"

Vicki stopped. "Are you kidding me? Who's Elaine? You don't even remember your twin sister?"

Mitch felt his knees grow weak. He braced himself against a wall. "I have a twin?"

"Yeah."

Mitch had often felt as though a part of him were missing. He was like a person without a shadow. But he had attributed that sense to the loneliness of having been raised as an only child. "What did she look like?"

"I can't recall, except for the curly blonde hair and the dimples. Oh, yeah. She had these big beautiful bluish-green eyes. Like the ocean. What color are your eyes?"

"Brown."

"Brown? Like me. Oh well."

"That's odd. Our mother spoke of you, but she never mentioned anything about any other kids. Why?"

Vicki hesitated. "I can't talk about it right now, Mitch. Sorry."

"But wait…" Mitch gripped the deadened phone.

*   *   *

At the Administration for Children's Services office the next morning, Mitch opened his records. He was amazed that only two children were taken from the Withers household on December 23, 1972. Mitch was not surprised to read that his home was destroyed by his mother's mental and physical abuse. Since visiting that old apartment, his mind had become engulfed with memories. Not the kind that warmed you in a daydream vision, but the kind that tortured your sleep with nightmares.

He called Vicki from his cellphone after leaving the Social Service offices. "I'd like you to meet Annabella. My daughter."

* * *

Vicki wore her best suit for the visit. The style had disappeared with the Big 80's, but soon her days of shopping at the Salvation Army would be over. She finally had a long-lost relative who was rich.

As she bounced from foster home to foster home, she had wished for a moneyed relative to surface. It finally became apparent that Daddy Warbucks was not coming to the rescue. Vicki realized that her best shot was to find a wealthy husband. But of all the successful lawyers in New York City to marry, she had to choose the one with a gambling problem. Whatever money he had made, she had not seen. It all went to Lucky Lucy or Whirlwind Wanda.

The divorce had been costly, leaving her with not much more than the few clothes in her closet. Soon she would not have a closet to store them in. The eviction was set for next week.

She pressed the doorbell to Mitch's penthouse apartment on the corner of East 89th and Lexington. My, how she loved heights. And closet space.

The door opened almost immediately. Vicki thought she was staring into a mirror. The resemblance between her and her brother was uncanny.

"I guess we must have looked like Dad," said Mitch.

Vicki nodded. "Mother had the blonde hair. And the blue/green eyes."

Mitch led Vicki through the foyer into the library. Crystal chandeliers illuminating damask walls awed her. The ceilings were tall and the views outstretching. Why couldn't some millionaire family have adopted her?

At least now she had her well-to-do brother. After accepting his offer of tea, Vicki relaxed on a brocade sofa.

"What a pretty cup and saucer. They even match," she said, the fragile china rattling in her tenuous grasp. Cocktail time was overdue. She hoped her edginess was not too obvious.

"Thank you. Vicki, the reason I…"

The little girl appeared, tossing her bright curls. She fastened her large eyes onto Vicki.

"Annabella. It's not polite to stare." Mitch shrugged at his sister. "Say hello to your Aunt Vicki." The little girl revealed dimples that eclipsed her smile.

Vicki was speechless, unnerved by the girl.

"Vicki, are you all right?" said Mitch.

"S-she looks just like...Elaine."

Mitch stopped. "I need to know about Elaine. Children's Services have no record of her having ever been taken from our mother's home. Vicki, what happened to Elaine?"

Vicki's arm trembled. Her teacup crashed to the floor. She yelled and jumped from the sofa. The little girl fled from the room.

"I-I don't know, Mitch. I've blocked out so much from my mind about those days. Sorry about the cup." She knelt down, picking up the broken shards.

"Tell me what you remember. Please. I've been wracking my mind."

Vicki gripped a piece of the china, nearly cutting her hand. "Screams, torture. I saw a shrink to help me get over this, Mitch. I take medicine to help me forget."

"But don't you see that we have to find Elaine? That's why I invited you here. You say Annabella looks like Elaine. Our mother went berserk when she saw Annabella.

Something isn't right. What happened the last time you saw Elaine?"

Vicki shook her head, tears of mascara streaking her skin. She blew her nose. "Get me a scotch. Please."

He poured a glass of Pinch while Vicki dug through her purse for a pack of Marlboros and bottle of Valium. She popped a couple of pills with her scotch and lit a cigarette. She hated her mind-numbing dependency. But it was better than reality.

Far better.

"So you do medicate." He handed her a crystal ashtray.

"You do what you gotta do to get by. You wouldn't know about that. Life's been lucky for you, little brother. Way lucky." Vicki chugged the rest of her scotch and held out her glass. Mitch refilled it. His sister was right. He had been lucky. Her misfortune could be read in the dark pouches and lines of her face that the make-up did not disguise.

Vicki crushed her cigarette into the ashtray. "I need a place to stay." She glanced around. "And I'm feeling pretty comfortable here."

"I can help you, if you help me. Now go on. Tell me," he said.

Vicki squeezed her eyes shut. "Elaine was in the bathtub screaming because the water was so hot and getting hotter.

She wouldn't stop crying and I was crying cause I didn't know how to turn the water off and Mama said if we didn't shut up, she'd whip us both. Mama didn't have much patience for crying. I hated it when Elaine cried. It made me scared.

"Mama came running in the room, started flipping out. Then I saw baby Elaine with her face down, floating in the water. Don't you remember, Mitch?"

He shrugged. "Why should I remember?"

"You were there."

Mitch sank into a nearby chair.

"You blacked it out same as me. That's why when the pictures come back in my head, I shut them away with these."

Vicki rattled the bottle of Valium before dropping it back in her purse. "I never saw Elaine again after that. Couple days later, those ladies showed up at our apartment and took us. Mama had the Christmas music cranked up on the radio. Guess so she wouldn't have to hear any more crying." Vicki stifled a sob. "It was playing 'Silent Night.'"

Mitch grabbed his phone and dialed.

"Who are you calling?"

"The police. That woman—our mother—is hiding something."

*   *   *

Her front door shook from the impact of fists beating against it.

"Who's there?" Miss Withers called out.

"It's the police. Open up."

The police? She glanced around, but there was no place to hide. Why should she hide? For twenty-five years, she had been waiting for this day. Then her only choice was to surrender Vicki and Mitchell. She had prayed that Children's Services would separate them into different households. She had not wanted Mitch to suffer the same fate his twin had at the hands of their older sibling.

Vicki had been jealous of Elaine since the day she was born. Vicki beating on her baby sister, causing her to howl in pain, was worse than any sibling rivalry. It was a prelude to murder.

The day Vicki wanted to help bathe Elaine, her mother had doubts. But Vicki was a willful child. How often since that tragic day had Miss Withers wished she'd trusted her instincts instead of Vicki. How long had Miss Withers left the bathroom where Elaine played in the tub with Vicki kneeling on the floor next to her? Seconds, minutes?

Hearing cries, she ran into the room, the scalding bath burning her hands as she lifted Elaine's limp body from under the water. Little Mitch crouched in a corner, shivering underneath a towel. "It was an accident," Vicki had screamed, though there was a look of triumph in her face.

Foster care was much better for Vicki than juvenile hall. Even if it meant lying to the authorities that she was abusive and unfit, Miss Withers would not let the law have Vicki. As a mother, she had to protect her child.

The police continued to pound at the door. "We have a search warrant."

She heard someone fumbling with the lock and the voice of the building manager. She stood there, frozen, as Grogan let the two policemen inside.

Grogan said nothing to her. He followed the detectives as they began to open doors and drawers, rifling through her belongings.

"You got a key for this door?" said one detective, trying a closet.

Grogan scowled at the old woman he always believed was crazy. The ring of keys fastened to his belt jangled as he searched through his collection. He shook his head.

"Miss Withers, where is the key?" said the detective, not too kindly. She sat in her rocker, wrapped in a comforter, humming "Silent Night."

The two detectives shrugged at each other. Then a booted leg kicked apart the door from its frame, much to Grogan's displeasure. He would bill the repairs to the City of Brooklyn.

Inside, the closet was dark and crammed with boxes. Shoved to the back was an old aluminum Christmas tree, decorations and garland still clinging to its flimsy branches. One detective pulled out the boxes while the other opened them, dumping out the contents.

The old woman continued to rock, faster now. A shriek from across the room did not stop her. She continued to rock and hum.

"Oh, Mother, God in Heaven." Grogan collapsed to the floor.

In a small trunk, lined with cellophane and air fresheners, was the small, mummified body of a three-year-old girl. She was wrapped in pink baby blankets and plastic bags. Beside her lay a copy of a newspaper, dated December 21, 1976.

Miss Withers felt the cold metal clamp around her wrists. She stopped rocking and humming long enough to hear her rights as the detective read them. She let him lead her from the chair and out of the apartment. She sighed with relief. The baby had stopped crying.

*   *   *

Vicki had hoped her arrangement with Mitch would be more permanent. But the few weeks she had stayed at his apartment and gotten smashed on his expensive scotch had convinced him otherwise. Searching for a place in Manhattan, Vicki found housing expensive and unavailable. Except for one unit that was on the market and cheap, by New York City standards.

Her mother's apartment.

Grogan was eager to fill the vacancy, and Mitch had prepaid a year's worth of the rent with the condition that Vicki enter a rehab program. That Vicki had aided in the arrest of her mother was a bonus, in Grogan's opinion. Now he could finally welcome a good night's rest.

*   *   *

"Yeah." He answered the telephone, his voice crusty with sleep.

"Mr. Grogan. The baby won't stop crying. It's driving me crazy."

"Ach, Mrs. Vicki. It's three-thirty in the morning. Go back to bed. The nightmare is over."

"Yeah, Mr. Grogan. But for some of us, it's only the beginning."

Toast

By Rex Brooke

Henry shuffled into the kitchen, unearthed a cup from the drainboard midden, and poured a cold cup of three day old coffee. He slipped the cup into the microwave, hit 90 seconds on high, and sat down to wait for enlightenment.

A ray of sunlight angled in through the kitchen window, and like a jaundiced ghost, slowly crawled across the food-crusted floor. Henry dragged the cup out of the microwave and blew gently across the foaming surface, setting it on the envelope of the pay-or-quit order from the landlord. Vaporous cobras of moisture undulated into the air. Henry blew his nose. He stood at the sink, took his first sip, and looked out the window to where Mr. Ota was backing his exhausted Cadillac out his driveway. Henry had lived for two years across the street from Mr. Ota, and had never spoken to him.

He picked up the document and looked at the dates. Shouldn't be a problem. They had to give them at least 30 days. And Kasmir had told him he would have some money coming in. "Lots of money," he said. "First you get the money, then you get the power. Then you get the woman." Yeah, baby.

Henry turned to the kitchen clock. 8:32 a.m., which meant it was really 6:17 a.m. He took another sip, bigger this time, with just enough substance to scald his tongue and ignite the growing cavity in his top right molar. He was hungry. Had he not had dinner the night before? He couldn't remember yet. A half-filled plate in the refrigerator helped begin to fill in the details. Kasmir, his Indian roommate, had made some kind of potato curry. He was all a-twitter about some fabulous breakthrough he had made. Something about debunking the singularity theory that a thing could only be in one place at one time. Kasmir went on and on about how a thing could be (and was) in all places at all times, and blah blah quantum tunnelings and the separation of the time space continuum. Whatever. Henry never understood much of what Kasmir was raving about. The guy was not right in the head. He thought that everyone on Earth had been sent here, back from the dead, to wander the Earth looking for their true self. And his cooking was indigestible, even after two glasses of vodka.

What to eat, what to eat…cereal? A box of Multigrain heart-benefiting oat-something. God he wished he had a girlfriend. Stupid. What girl would want to be with him? His last date, three months before, had been a total disaster.

Felicia. She was hot. Oh well. He held the cereal box up to the light. No moth larvae spinning webs in the wrapping. That was good. He shook out a bowlful, and hauled out the half gallon of milk, which plopped out of the carton in lumps of white diarrhea. He dumped the contents of the bowl into the sink, and tried flushing the clotted mix down the drain. When the water began to back up into the sink, he turned on the garbage disposal. It groaned, but did not grind. After a few seconds it began to smoke. Henry switched it back off.

It was then that Henry noticed the toaster. Polished steel with black handles. A floral design etched on one side. Had it been there before? It certainly wasn't like the usual junk Kasmir kept. He had a roomful of broken computers and scrap metal machinery--transformers, gears, copper windings, magnets, diodes, rectifiers, cathode ray tubes, tiny speakers. And a sitar, which was missing several strings which, when properly lubricated with alcohol, Kasmir could partially play, even if it was just the one Bob Dylan song. But nothing as useful as a toaster.

Henry got a piece of bread from out of the cupboard, and peeled off the part of the crust that had mold on it. He unplugged the microwave and plugged the toaster into the one electrical outlet that didn't light up like a Las Vegas nightclub when he tried to use it. He carefully slid the bread into one of the open slots, and pushed the black handle down.

"Ouch!"

Henry looked about the room.

"Hot! Too much kinetic energy! Stop, I am deploring you."

What the hell? It was Kasmir's voice, but where was Kasmir?

"Stop, mother bastard!"

The voice was coming from the toaster. Henry popped up the untoasted bread. A panting noise came from inside-- Henry peered down the bread slot into the zig-zagging metal wires.

"Kasmir? Where are you man?"

"Here in I am, most unfortunately."

Henry turned the toaster around, looking for a microphone. He unplugged the toaster.

"Really Kasmir. This is cool." He left the kitchen and went to Kasmir's bedroom. Fucking Bengali. Always screwing around with machines. The mattress on the floor was unmade, but then Kasmir never made his bed. The window was open, and the sheet which Kasmir used as a curtain was trembling in the morning breeze. A disemboweled computer spread its intestines across the floor. On the desk, a large aluminum bread box with wires going in and out of it hummed a white noise lullaby.

Henry looked in the restroom.

He looked in the closet.

Where the hell was he?

He went back into the kitchen and looked at the toaster.

He shook it. Nothing.

"Come on, man. How'd you do it?"

He plugged the toaster back in.

"No. The exit access. Do not interrupt, please," came Kasmir's voice.

"OK. I won't. Where are you? This is great."

"This am I. An improbability has become probable. Ten thousand angels on the head of a pin have tipped the entropy of the universe."

"Boy, that's good news. Maybe we can pay the rent now. Great gag, Kasmir. Really. So where are you?"

"I am this, my dear Henry. Quantized. The on and off has become on or off. You must assist."

Henry turned the toaster over and opened up the door on the bottom.

"Stop!" the toaster giggled.

Henry snapped the door back down and righted the toaster. There was no speaker embedded inside.

"OK. This is good. You must be streaming this live from somewhere remotely. Somewhere. I've got it. Drone. But why the voice from the toaster? This is really good, Kasmir."

"It is most certainly no joke, Henry. I am here."

"You're in a toaster?"

"I am at one a toaster."

Henry sat down on one of the metal folding chairs. "Where are you really?"

"I am really saying this to you truly."

"Shit, Kasmir."

"Yes shit, Henry. Very much shit. Unknown to me, electron dissimilator reversed its polarity. The inevitable possibility of spontaneity."

"Not giving up, are you? Well, I'd love to stay and chat with you all day," Henry said, getting to his feet, "but I've got to get to work." Henry was a substitute math teacher at various middle schools. He reached to unplug the toaster.

"No. Please. Do not unplug the. . ." pleaded Kasmir's voice.

"Really?" Henry unplugged the toaster, and plugged the microwave back in. He grabbed a banana from the over-ripe bunch which was fathering a cloud of fruit flies, and unlocked the front door. "See you tonight," he said glancing around the room for a video camera.

There was no reply. Henry hesitated at the door, and then left.

* * *

Henry returned at 3:30 that afternoon, after a rather taxing day at an inner city middle school. It was his first time at that school, and the hormonally challenged teens had a field day. In first period, he sent a group of five boys to the counselor, who promptly sent them back with a note telling him to please keep the children in class. Second period, a fight broke out in the back of the room between a boy and a girl, which everyone videotaped for posting on the internet. By third period Henry had given up attempting to get the students to do the four page assignment the absent teacher had left for them, and let the students play on their cell phones for the entire period. One of the girls, who was remarkably well developed for a seventh grader, wanted him to friend her on Facebook. Consequently, the first thing that Henry did when he got home was to pour a water glass full of Vodka of the Gods, and knock it back in two gulps. A 7th grader. He leaned against the counter and looked out to watch Mr. Ota pull into his driveway, the twin tailpipes smoking like a Pennsylvania steel mill. He then turned his attention to the toaster.

Henry plugged the toaster in and sat down to watch it. When nothing happened, he stood, picked the toaster up, smelled it, shook it gently, and put his ear to the slot for the bread. He could hear snoring. At least it sounded like someone snoring. It was probably some sort of weird echo, resonance thing, vibrating sympathetically to the hum of the refrigerator. He pushed the handle down and watched the coil of wires begin to glow red.

"Mothafuka! Hot sonofabitch!"

Henry popped the handle up. The toaster continued to pant.

"Hey, Kasmir," Henry said in a suddenly buoyant mood. "How's it going? What's cooking?"

"Finally you have returned. Henry. My friend. Do make jokes. You must assist me in this most puzzling of dilemmas."

"Certainly. What can I do for you, you demented fakir?"

"Reverse the polarity on the transaxial potention coil."

"Right. Whatever. No problem."

"Serious, Henry. In my room. You will find it. Flip polarity. Blue to red and red to blue. Get me out of here. Quickly Henry. I am afraid I am leaking into randomness."

"Right."

"Please. I am begging you."

"Whatever. You're leaking into randomness? Get some Depends."

Henry poured another glass of vodka and sauntered into Kasmir's room. "So you're in here somewhere." There was no answer. On the desk, Henry began to examine the aluminum breadbox. Inside was a strange arrangement of tubes, diodes, capacitors and other gadgets that looked like something out of a Frankenstein movie. It continued to hum as he carefully touched the maze of wires. They were warm. He traced the wires back to the voltage source, and unplugged the red, positive wire. The humming stopped.

"Idiot," Henry muttered. "Going to burn this place down."

The wires emerged from a smaller metal box and terminated in two metal handles. One red. One blue. He took a large gulp of vodka, set the glass down and carefully grabbed the handles. Nothing. He unplugged the blue negative wire, and connected it to the positive electrode. Still nothing. He reconnected the positive wire, to the negative electrode, and grabbed the handles again. This time he disappeared.

In the kitchen, the red burner light on the stove suddenly blinked on. "What the fuck?" Henry's voice echoed out of the oven.

"Nice," said the toaster. "Now what do we do?"

"What happened?" asked a panicked stovetop.

"I will tell you, you ignorant bag of hammers. You have failed in the most simple of operations. I told you: reverse the polarity on the quantum wormhole generator. Now we are both this."

"I did reverse the fucking polarity. Where am I? Where are my hands? My feet?" whined Henry.

"You too have entered into the world of quantum electrodynamics. We travel as organized particle waves through wires until we reach an outlet. If the outlet has an appliance, we can partially re-enter the physical world as most people know it."

"So you really are a toaster..."

"And you, my friend, are a manly four burner oven. With electronic ignition."

"I don't feel very manly," Henry replied, turning on one of this burners and then snapping it back off. "What now?"

"Now we must await for good fortune of someone to come into our apartment. A someone who can follow the most simple of instructions."

"I'm sorry," said Henry. "I did reverse the wires, though."

"You are sure?"

"I am sure."

"I see," said the toaster.

"You do? I don't see a thing. Maybe this is all an illusion. Wake up! Wake up!" Henry yelled at himself. The burners rattled back.

"No my dear Henry. This is not an illusion. We are talking. Therefore we are."

The toaster hummed, and then continued. "Heads or tails, Henry. Heads or tails?"

"What?"

"You flip a coin, 50-50 chance heads or tails, right? But if it lands heads five times in a row, is the next flip still 50-50?"

"You wouldn't think so."

"But it is. Probability has no memory. And yet it does."

"I wish I could forget this."

"It is simple quantum electrodynamics, man," Kasmir continued before suddenly shouting, "Holy shit mother bastard! We are most certainly leaking."

"What?"

"Leaking! Entropy! Someone must need to be very soon here. We must be able to pee up the fire hose of chaos. We need that dancing angel. We need help!"

And with that, the two roommates began to yell for help, but like the falling tree in the forest, no one could hear them. After half an hour of shouting, they fell silent. Over the next several hours, now and then, they would suddenly, spontaneously, again start yelling for help. Then the yelling would disperse into a conversation about their childhood, or they would sing a Bob Dylan song to which they knew some of the words, or Kasmir would speculate more about the nature of the material world, or of the question of mind over matter and the transmigration of the soul. Eventually they would lapse back into silence. Over the ensuing week, the silences gradually became longer and longer, the pleas for help became more and more truncated until all they could do is whisper "angel, angel," as the nights and days blinked on and off.

Three weeks later, the apartment door banged open and a twenty something woman entered, dragging in a bucket of rags and a mop. She dropped the cleaning tools into a pile, closed the door, sat down on the couch, lit a joint, and pulled out her cell phone and made a call.

"It looks like they just left everything here. What do you want me to do with all this stuff? Throw it out? All of it? OK. This is going to take a few days. Fine." She closed up the phone and dropped it into her purse. She took another hit from her joint and sat back, watching the twisting smoke float out of her mouth.

"Excuse me. Hello. Yes. You there. You must not be doing such a thing," announced Kasmir. Henry awoke and rattled his front burner.

The young woman quickly put out the joint. "What the hell?" On her left arm was a long tattoo in Gothic letters: "Trust No Man."

"Your clear head must have. You."

The woman looked anxiously around the room. "What the hell? Who are you? Where are you?"

"I am Kasmir, pleased to meet of you again."

"Kasmir! My uncle said he evicted you."

"No, no, no. I am here. We are here. Both of us."

"Where? Where the fuck are you?"

Kasmir sucked the handle down on the toaster, and then popped it back up. "I am here! Toaster machine. Please. Kind beautiful lady. You must assist us in this most unusual predicament."

The woman cautiously approached the toaster and looked down into its coils. "Right."

"Please, kind lady."

"They warned me this was going to happen. 'Felicia,' they said, 'you gotta quit on that shit. Yourbrain gonna be fried egg on toast.' Holy Miss Moses. I've done it now."

"In the bedroom. There is a box."

"Stop! Just stop! No voices. No voices." Felicia put her hands over her ears.

"There is an aluminum box. Two handles."

"I can't hear you." Felicia began to sing the Star Bangled Hammer:

"Jose can you see, by the dog's . . ."

"Felicia!" shouted the stovetop.

"Holy shit. Holy shit! I'm out of here."

"Wait! Felicia! It's me Henry. Wait. Please. You remember me. We met before, when your uncle rented this place to us. We went out on a date. You were wearing a Dodger jersey, and daisy dukes."

"You are supposed to not be here."

"There's been a problem."

"Worst date I've ever been on…"

"Yes, yes, well…sorry about that. I thought you'd be interested in..."

"In going to the zoo? To depressed, threadbare animals living in cages? Ha. I can see that downtown anytime. Really."

"Again, sorry."

"Worst date I've ever been on."

"Yes. You made that perfectly clear. But listen, Felicia. A terrible accident has happened, and we - Kasmir and me – we are…we're trapped in these appliances."

"Isn't that a shame…I'll be right back. Or maybe not." Felicia opened the door.

"Wait!" shouted the toaster. "Get us out of here and I will make you a rich woman."

Felicia hesitated, turned, and slowly closed the door. She strolled back into the kitchen. "Talk to me, toaster boy."

Five minutes later, Felicia, bolstered by promises of shared copyright income, was poised in front of the aluminum lunch box, listening to Kasmir calling out the instructions from the kitchen for the fifth time.

"Red to red. Blue to blue. Connect the blue first. Connect the blue first," Kasmir yelled.

"I heard you the first time."

"You've reversed the leads," Henry whispered anxiously to Kasmir.

"We cannot predetermine if the polarity has flipped. Right now the cat is both alive and dead."

"What cat?"

"Schrodinger's."

"There's a cat in the box?"

"Do you know nothing? Quite simply it is a crappy shot. Heads and tails becomes heads or tails."

"Blue is connected," called Felicia from the bedroom. "Connecting the red."

There was a long pause. "Connecting the…"

There was a flash of light. The refrigerator door swung open and closed. "What the fuck?" came Felicia's voice from somewhere near the meat drawer. "Where the hell am I? It's fucking cold in here."

"The polarity was not flipped," whispered Kasmir. "I am thus concluding."

"Get me the fuck out of here! I'm fucking freezing."

"Felicia," Henry said with an oven's firmness in his voice, "open your door. I will warm you."

"Right."

"Trust me."

"I don't think so."

"OK. Don't trust me. But open your door."

After several seconds, the door to the refrigerator slowly swung open. Henry lit all four burners, turned them on high, and, for good measure, fired up his broiler.

"Ahhh," cooed Felicia. "That is nice. Thank you." The refrigerator light cast a yellow halo. "But the ice is melting. I'm getting all wet."

In the kitchen, the toaster coughed. "We'll worry about that later," Henry said nonchalantly. He was, quite literally, glowing. "We have lots of time. Someone else will come rescue us." He turned his burners down a notch, and listened, with something akin to rapture, to the purring refrigerator.

*   *   *

Outside, at the corner gas station, a threadbare man bought 10 Lotto tickets, returned to his truck, and sitting in the driver's seat, uttered a prayer to the Virgin of Guadalupe. He then began, with a quarter, to scratch off the numbers.

Jikan

by Joan Brown

Beyond the known universe, in a never-ending cluster of stars and moons and other celestial bodies, revolves tiny Jikan — a planet of possibilities wondrous and horrendous. At one extreme pole of Jikan, at the apex of time and space, stands a round villa with a flat roof. On the roof is an open-air pavilion. And this is where Syzygy entertains.

Covering the pavilion is a white canopy intricately embroidered with multiple shades of greens, browns, and golds, in the design of a magnificent pinecone swirling into infinity. Under this mystical canopy, along the south side, on a fuchsia and chartreuse paisley patterned velveteen cushion, sits Syzygy.

"Where is he?" Syzygy asks. "Why is he always late? Why do I even care?" Thinking about what she just said, she groans. "Now I'm even thinking like him."

"If that's so," Marcel says, "just kill yourself now."

"This torment is its own death," she laughs, "Or its own life."

Hating philosophy, and totally not caring one way or another, Marcel, on his perch, preens and smirks. "He's probably lost somewhere between here and Pluto. That piece-of-junk space saucer he flies doesn't have a Galactical Positioning System."

Deviously smiling, Syzygy says, "And neither does Rinkus have a time piece," and reaching under her fuchsia and chartreuse paisley patterned velveteen cushion, she pulls out a precious chronometer.

Marcel bobs and wolf-whistles. "How did you get that? Did you steal it?"

"What do you think it's worth to him to get it back?"

"You're in love with Rinkus."

"How could I possibly be in love with some so utterly ugly when I am so divinely gorgeous?"

In his nasally parrot voice, Marcel snort-laughs. "Right! In your sleep, I hear you moaning for him."

"You lie!"

"I never lie," Indignantly Marcel stomps his taloned foot on the wooden perch. "Ohhh, Rinkus, Rinkus, tell me you love me as I love you," he laughs in the same fashion Rinkus does. "Besides, why else did you get this new-fangled table?"

Turning every jewel color in the unknown world, Syzygy throws a kalpolly cherry at him.

"Ohh, darling, don't think I don't feel for you."

Syzygy opens her mouth to ask when it was he could ever have been in love, but she changes her mind and shuts up.

"Proust tells us there are only three important things in life," Stretching to the east Marcel listens. "Here he comes."

Even though Syzygy can't hear anything yet, she re-hides Rinkus' precious possession under her fuchsia and chartreuse paisley-patterned velveteen cushion. "Where's Havila?"

"Downstairs."

Spreading his wings and lifting off, Marcel flies over the top of the new-fangled table, out of the pavilion and east over the vegetable gardens. Gliding downwards, he lands, hidden, somewhere in one of the orchards.

Behind where Syzygy sits, on the south side of the pavilion, growing up from the surface of Jikan, are heady-scented kalpolly trees with thick, gnarly limbs, and smooth berries. Rooted and spilling from the top of the kalpolly, and entangled in its leaves and limbs, are bougainvillea vines sporting abundant arrays of orange and yellow blossoms.

To the north, straight in front of where Syzygy sits, is her favorite view — Jikan's great rings of midnight blue and neon pink continuously vibrating and pulsing, stretching and reaching into the void.

Rinkus' space saucer, flying in from the east, over the top of the orchards and vegetable gardens, booms and rattles the pavilion then lands with a loud clank on the west side saucer pad.

Downstairs, Havila leaves her haunt, crosses the kitchen, and goes out. Behind her, the screen door slaps shut.

Rinkus smiles as he turns to face her. "Always good to see you, Havila."

Forever feeling the weight of the world, Havila almost never smiles, and doesn't now. "She's waiting for you upstairs."

Sweetly, even though the heat makes him sweat like a three-gutted boar, Rinkus asks, "Any chance of an icy pitcher of ambrosia?"

"Are you not always served ambrosia when you visit?"

"Yes, definitely. You're the best hostess ever, but I don't want to be presumptuous."

Irritated, Havila glares at him.

"What smells so good?"

Havila flicks her hand toward the outside stairs that go from Jikan's surface to the villa on the rooftop.

Upstairs, under the canopy, Syzygy checks to make sure the precious chronometer is well hidden before she smooths her dress, touches her jewelry, and corrects her posture. Heart pounding, she listens to the scuff-flop, scuff-flop of Rinkus' sandals on the stair steps.

Emerging with his bristly orange hair glinting in the sun — to his kaftan of aqua blue with silver arabesque — and finally his big, seven-toed feet, Rinkus asks, "Am I late?"

Sweeter than pokolinny pie, Syzygy smiles. "Late? How would I know? I'm not the one who keeps track of the time."

"My chronometer is missing."

"You've lost your precious timepiece?"

He squints at her.

"Please, come have a seat in the shade of the canopy, and tell me what took you so long."

Cross because he's hot and doesn't like flying, in addition to getting lost on the way over, Rinkus snaps.

"What do you mean?"

"What do you mean what do I mean? You're always saying I don't try and see things from your point of view, so I was putting myself into your frame of mind."

"Now you're a mind reader?"

"You just got here and you're already making me cross-eyed," Syzygy glares at him then points to the far side of the table.

"Please, have a seat and make yourself comfy."

Sprawling in an overstuffed loveseat, Rinkus looks around the pavilion. "So you finally got your new-fangled table."

Syzygy leans forward. "Look at its cutting edge design. I had it made special."

"You've only told me that a hundred times."

"Watch this." Grabbing hold of the edge, she gives a lift and a twist, and waits expectantly.

Nothing happens.

Rinkus grins.

Syzygy gives the table a jerk and a yank.

Nothing happens.

Grinning, Rinkus sits back and folds his hands over his massively bulbous and beautiful belly.

With a hard grunt and all her might, Syzygy tries again.

Nothing happens.

She glares at Rinkus expectantly.

He grins at her.

She snaps, "Could you give me a hand?'

Biting his tongue to keep from laughing out loud, Rinkus leans forward and takes hold of the table. "Love to."

"You're an ass."

Underneath the table, the floor opens to reveal a shallow, but spacious pit filled with dried kalpolly and fir logs.

"Is that your new heating system?"

"No, it's my new incinerator for rude guests."

"That's what you had to have special made?"

"The top turns into a game board," she leans back, "and there's one more function I'll show you later."

"You surprise me," Rinkus says.

What do you mean?"

"All your long speeches about time being circular and nothing ever being really new and how you think gross commercialism promotes rabid inequality, yet you're proud as Pandora with her unopened box."

"You're a complete and ignorant ass."

Rinkus laughs, but his eyes bore into Syzygy.

"Do you want to play Resources?" she asks.

"Of course. You know I love destruction, misery and killing."

They hear the kitchen screen door slap shut, then quiet steps traveling the stairs.

Havila emerges carrying a tray with two amethyst goblets, a pitcher of tinkling ice floating in ambrosia, and two malachite dishes piled with biscuits.

Rinkus says, "There's that something that smells divine."

"Maybe they'll be your new favorite," Havila says.

"What are they?" Rinkus asks.

"That's for me to know and you to think about."

"Are you going to play Resources with us?" Syzygy asks.

"No."

"What else do you have to do?" Rinkus asks.

"Whatever else I want."

Rinkus says, "Whatever it is, you can do later. It's not like you're on a time limit."

"I am when it comes to getting out to the garden and digging parsnips before they rot in the ground."

Nodding righteously, Rinkus says to Syzygy, "Havila knows, time is a physical process, a relation between consciousness and the rotation of suns and stars across the sky."

"The key word is rotation," Syzygy says. "Birth, maturing and dying are easily observable, and it's as easily observable that it's a constant and repeating cycle. Therefore, one second, one day, one lifetime is no more or less meaningful than the next. Different, yet the same."

Rinkus flops back. "Every fool knows time moves ever forward. Celestial bodies may spin, but time goes forward — in a straight line."

"Not so," Syzygy insists. "The electrical impulses of minds, the transference of energy in roots and limbs of plants, the synaptic connections of celestial bodies, they're all the same." She takes a biscuit and starts munching.

"That's ridiculous. That's like saying life and death are the same."

"It's simply a barrier of mind."

Havila fills the amethyst goblets with ambrosia. "Let me know what you think of the biscuits." Turning, she disappears down the stairs.

After smelling a biscuit, Rinkus takes a bite. His eyes brighten. A big crumb drops from his mouth and onto his aqua blue and silver arabesque kaftan. Tucking up his chin, he glances down, finds what he's looking for, and pops it in his mouth.

"You're a slob."

"I don't care," he shrugs, grinning.

"I wish you would act your age."

"Hah!" Rinkus laughs.

Syzygy's eyebrows crunch closer together. "Hah, what?"

"By admitting to age, you admit time is linear."

"Absolutely not."

"But you cannot deny that everything ages."

"You cannot deny that everything renews."

Across the new-fangled table, Syzygy and Rinkus glare at each other.

Usually she's all for a good fight and cannot control her selfish impulses and damn the consequences, but today she shuts her mouth, sits back, and rethinks what she truly wants.

Ambrosia tastes like mango, honeysuckle and ginger, and sunrays on crisp cool air tingling over a fresh bubbling brook. After a long drink, Rinkus closes his eyes as he relaxes into the overstuffed loveseat. "Aaahh." Head tilted back and wearing a goofy smile, he reopens his eyes to stare into the infinity of the huge pinecone of the canopy swirling greens into browns into golds, seemingly forming and reforming.

Syzygy gazes past Rinkus into Jikan's great midnight blue and neon pink rings, vibrating and pulsing, stretching further and further.

Suddenly, though, her conscious is snapped back to right here, right now. Her heart leaps at the howls of the killer

"YOOOUUUUU, YEAH, YOOOOUUUU."

Carried in the howls are fears of the unknown. Piercing notes echo yearnings imagined and dreaded, of not getting enough, of not being enough, of being afraid to die. It howls and stalks and obliterates then leaves the carcasses to rot as it stews in its own desires. Hovering, it is greedy to kill again, "YOOOUUUUU, YEAH, YOOOOUUUU."

Rinkus sits up. "Where's Marcel?" He shivers. "The killer sounds close."

Bracelet and anklets tingling, Syzygy, careful not to let her fuchsia and chartreuse paisley patterned velveteen cushion shift, stands and walks to the east edge of the roof. Using her hand to shade her eyes from the sun, she looks for Marcel.

From the west comes the thundering of four and six legged beasties stampeding. Beyond the edge of the field, in the forest, flocks of birds make a cacophony and rise into the lilac sky. Again the killer, consumed with fear and hate and anger, howls.

"YOOOUUUUU, YEAH, YOOOOUUUU."

Syzygy folds her arms around herself.

Relief in his voice, Rinkus announces, "There's Marcel." He leaves the overstuffed loveseat to go and stand on the roof's edge with Syzygy.

Over the orchards and gardens, Marcel flies swift and piercing as an arrow, tucking and gliding he swoops under the canopy and lands on his perch. "Is it lunch time?"

Rinkus, on the way back to the overstuffed loveseat, says, "You can't trick me."

Pivoting on his perch to face south, Marcel ignores him.

Syzygy, returning to her fuchsia and chartreuse paisley patterned velveteen cushion gets comfortable. "How do you like the biscuits?"

"Umm, delicious. What is this fruit in here? I'm sure I've tasted it somewhere else a long time ago."

"Hah!" Syzygy grins and glares. "That's impossible. Mélange grows only on Jikan."

Confused, Rinkus stares at Syzygy.

"Since, in your linear scheme of time, Jikan is a new planet, then mélange is a new tree."

"You and your stupid little syllogisms!"

Syzygy glares at Rinkus, and devours a biscuit.

Grinning back at her across the gaming table, Rinkus sips more ambrosia.

Marcel, concentrating on something in a tangle of vines, is stone still, and time stops.

Systematically popping one biscuit after another into mouth, Syzygy empties her malochite bowl. Licking her fingers, she asks, "Ready to play?"

Rinkus, with his mouth full, nods. As Syzygy opens the game box, Rinkus moves his still half-full plate of biscuits to where she cannot reach.

In the game box are two dice, a deck of 66 cards and five colors of sets of playing pieces. For each color, there are 1,000,000 beings with resources for one solar cycle. Usually Syzygy invites over other godlet gangsters to play, but she has decided she wants Rinkus to herself, so she simply sweeps away all colored beings except for her yellows and Rinkus' blues.

Gazing to the east, Rinkus sees Havila walking out with a gathering basket. Turning back to the table, he drinks more ambrosia, and notices that Marcel has remained still as a stone. At first, staring into the heady-smelling kalpolly trees and abundant bougainvillea vines and blossoms, he cannot see what Marcel is fixated on, but then he spies in the viney entanglement hundreds of tiny, baby decagons pushing their translucent, light-green legs through lighter green eggshells. Freeing themselves, they scurry for protection and nourishment.

Almost imperceptibly, Marcel shifts. His feathers are taut, talons ready to strike. He waits. Something lashes out, grabs two or three baby decagons, and munches. Marcel prickles; he will have that praying mantis.

"Hey," Syzygy says, "can you stop coveting the insect population and help me?"

"Honh?"

Pushing the spin-dial to him, she says, "Let's see what planet we get today."

It takes him a minute to get it figured out — he's not good with electronics — but finally a playing field appears on the new table. "It's ancient Earth."

"Oh, good," Syzygy takes a look. Smiling, she pushes to him his blue beings, and hoards her yellow beings. "I like all the resources and scattered land masses on Earth."

"I don't. There's too much water to have to get around."

"Makes for a strategic game."

Rinkus mumbles, "I like going in and simply destroying everyone and everything." He begins to enliven his blues and place them where he wants. "Any special or new rules?"

Busying animating her yellow beings, Syzygy shrugs.

"There aren't any?"

"Same as always."

"Of course." Done setting up, Rinkus rests his eyes on Syzygy.

She looks up.

He grins.

"I won last game, so you go first."

Picking up the dice, Rinkus blows on them for good luck.

"All your hocus pocus prayers didn't help you last game."

"Time changes everything."

"No, it doesn't. Everything revolves and evolves, but nothing truly changes."

"Crapola. If nothing ever changes than why isn't Earth a viable planet today?"

"But it will be again in another eon. And before it was the verdant habitation represented in this game, it was something else."

Rinkus lets loose the dice. "Nine." Using seven moves, he advances a force of 250,000 beings with resources to last six months across an ocean and into Syzygy's yellow territory. The remaining two moves he uses to buy a draw from the card pile. He hopes for a Major Disaster, but gets only a Small Disaster Card: five thousand dead, resources destroyed. Face down, he safe-keeps the card.

Leaning back on the overstuffed loveseat, Rinkus watches Syzygy, who always takes forever to complete her turn. He sips ambrosia, and the ice tinkles in his goblet.

Grabbing the dice, Syzygy smiles. Marcel turns and stares at Rinkus.

"What?"

He puffs up his feathers, stomps on his perch and imitates Rinkus being grumpy and aggressive.

Syzygy laughs. She loves throwing dice — that instant between throwing down and knowing. Flicking her wrist, she flares opens her palm. "Ten!"

Suddenly distracted, Marcel turns to face the tangle of vines and delicacies. Narrowing his focus, he glows with purpose.

Rinkus breathes deep the heady kalpolly, sips again from his amethyst goblet, and dreams of things he hasn't yet had. Cool ambrosia glows warm through his veins. Eyes wavering, they slide closed than back open, and he smiles dreamily.

With eight moves, Syzygy places two forces, 500,000 beings, with resources to last three months, halfway between her yellow base and where Rinkus has crossed his blue beings over the demarcation into her yellow territory. With her last two moves, she buys a draw, and gets an Annihilating Disease Card: kills 250,000, resources are transferred. She places it face down, off to one side.

Faster than thought, Marcel arrows into the tangle.

Syzygy and Rinkus hear the scream of death. "MEEEE, MEEE, MEEE."

When Marcel climbs out, he proudly picks from his beak the praying legs of the mantis.

Raising his hands and bowing in obeisance, Rinkus says, "Oh, mighty hunter."

Marcel laughs in perfect imitation of Syzygy.

Syzygy, reaching into the game box, hurls a screaming orange being at him.

Again, thundering sounds jerk their heads west where elk, antelope, and long limbed merbins are fleeing.

"YOOOUUUUU, YEAH, YOOOOUUUU."

When the beasties stop running, they try to eat, but their bodies bounce with blind instinct to not let go of the life they know.

Hyper-alert, Marcel sets down the leg of the mantis. To the east, Havila, her straw hat shading her face, looks toward the villa and beyond.

"YOOOUUUUU, YEAH, YOOOOUUUU."

Marcel listens for the echoes to die before flying away. Swooping low over Havila's head, he then rises and soars into the shadows of the orchard.

"MMMMEEEEE, MMMMEEEE, MMMMEE."

Jolted, startled, and sucking in his breath, Rinkus chokes on spit and biscuit. Explosively, he coughs and his face turns glaringly red.

"Rinkus," Syzygy squeaks struggling not to laugh, "you're gross."

Coughing and choking, his face turns from glaring to crimson and he doubles over.

"HAVILA," Syzygy screams. Jumping up, she runs around behind the overstuffed loveseat — where she cannot reach him. Running in front, she grabs his shoulders and shakes hard.

He sputters, gasps, convulses.

Havila hurries toward the villa.

WHAM

Syzygy slaps Rinkus hard on the back.

"Uuuufffff," Rinkus gasps and shudders.

WHAM

As hard as she can, she slams him again.

"AAaagghhhHH," he gasps — and gasps — and gasps.

Syzygy watches.

"MMMMEEEEE, MMMMEEEE, MMMMEE." From the west, another beastie screams in death.

Downstairs, the screen door slaps, and Havila runs up the stairs.

"Hoouuupp," Rinkus gasps. Now, drained of blood, his face is pale and his blue eyes are rimmed in pink and bugging out and dripping fluid. He falls and lays on his side while his breath grows bigger and calmer.

Havila, coming under the shade of the canopy, catches her own breath as she waits for Rinkus, the concern on her face turning to irritation.

When Rinkus finally sits up, he's still wet-eyed and feeble looking.

"How did this happen?" Havila demands.

Nothing moves, nothing peeps. The world spins in fear and glory.

Rinkus hoarsely asks, "Are you done with your roll?"

Syzygy leaves the overstuffed loveseat and returns to the south side and her fuchsia and chartreuse paisley patterned velveteen cushion.

Elk, antelope, and long-limbed merbins put their heads down to eat.

Marcel whistles.

Havila whistles.

Syzygy lets out her breath, and wishing she wouldn't hold it, takes in a big breath of heady kalpolly.

Rinkus drinks from his amethyst goblet.

"I'm going back to the parsnips," Havila says crossly.

"Love you too," Rinkus calls after her. Watching until her head disappears, Rinkus then grabs the dice, eyes the board, shakes and throws. "Five." He sits back on the overstuffed loveseat, gets a biscuit, and munching stares at the board.

He has one force of blue beings in yellow territory, and lined up against his blues are two yellow forces; all he rolled was a stinkin' five. Closing his eyes, Rinkus sips from his amethyst goblet.

"You're always complaining about me taking a long time, but you take longer."

Rinkus's eyes pop open, "Do not!"

"Do so!"

"If all time is renewing anyway, what do you care?"

"Yes," Syzygy says sitting up straight and tall, "well said."

Rinkus re-closes his eyes.

Having figured out a path of destruction, Rinkus re-opens his eyes and smiles. With two moves, he buys a draw and, luckily, gets a Nuclear Wipe-Out Card: destroys all within 250 kilometers, all resources lost. He puts it safely aside. With his remaining three moves, he advances from blue base another 50,000 beings, with resources for three months, across the water to yellow territory.

Pushing the dice toward Syzygy, he then sprawls back into the overstuffed loveseat.

In the north, the midnight blue and neon pink rings steadily vibrate and pulse. Syzygy likes staring at these rings; she doesn't know why, and she wonders if she should care that she doesn't know.

In the western fields, the animals eat, but are bouncy with caution. Wind gusts through the forest.

The killer howls, "YOOOUUUUU, YEAH, YOOOOUUUU."

To the east, Havila is waist deep in the vegetable garden.

Rinkus smiles at Syzygy.

She doesn't smile back.

His grin widens to be seemingly malicious.

Not taking her eyes off him, Syzygy reaches for the dice, feels their weight. Shaking her cupped hands and hovering them over the playing board, she lets loose. "Eleven."

Chewing on his biscuit, Rinkus starts choking.

"Not again!"

Turning left, away from Syzygy, red-faced Rinkus sees Havila coming with a basket on her hip and Marcel on her shoulder. He watches as they disappear under the eaves of the villa, then listens as the screen door slaps shut. "I'm fine now."

Thinking about her strategy, Syzygy sips ambrosia and wishes she had more biscuits, and while there probably are more downstairs, there's the constant danger of Havila's wrath. Plus she doesn't want to get fat. With seven moves, she advances 250,000 yellows with resources for a year toward her 500,000 advancing on Rinkus's blues. She spends two moves playing her Annihilating Disease Card. She recites, "Bulbous dead bodies, rotten and putrid virus, leaving none living," — and sweeps 250,000 blues off the game board. With her final two moves, she buys a draw from the card pile, and gets a Civil War Card: kills 100,000 and destroys resources. She tucks it out of sight.

Crippled from his loss, Rinkus squints at the board. He needs to roll at least an eight. He shakes the dice, then casts them across the playing board. "Five"

Joyfully, Syzygy claps her hands.

With all five moves, Rinkus advances from home base another blue force of 250,000 with three months of resources to join the remaining 50,000 beings in yellow territory. In his blue home base, he's only got 450,000 beings left, but he's got abundant resources.

Syzygy takes up the dice. "With a twelve, I could almost wipe you out."

"I'm betting you won't get a twelve."

Holding her breath, Syzygy is unsure of what to hope for. Indecision ignites the dice and they burn in her hand. She loves to win, but when the game is over, Rinkus always goes home. She lets go. "Six."

"Ha, ha."

She asks herself, "Am I relieved?"

Using four moves, she evacuates the yellow base and moves 250,000 beings with all her remaining resources, joining up with her previously advanced force of 250,000, giving her two forces of 500,000 beings. She buys a draw — and gets a Gang War and Criminal Dissension Card: kills 25,000 with resources confiscated.

"Twelve!" Rinkus yells.

"You cheat."

He laughs at her. "Suspicion thrives in the mind of the guilty." Gleefully, he crosses the water with 250,000 beings plus resources to join up with his 300,000 in yellow territory. Then he buys a draw — and gets a Fire Card: destroys 50,000 and all resources.

"Ten," Syzygy says. With eight moves, she combines all of her yellow forces and resources. Confident in her strong position, she uses her last two moves to play her Gang Wars and Criminal Dissension Card: "What you have, I want:

never ending fight for gain, hating, and killing." She sweeps 25,000 blue beings off the board and assumes the resources. "You're losing bad."

Rinkus rolls, "Five." With two moves, he plays his Fire Card. "High flame's screaming heat, all devouring appetite, nothing left to eat." He sweeps away 50,000 yellow beings with resources. With his final two moves, he buys a draw — and gets an Earthquake Card: kills 75,000, resources lost.

"Ten," Syzygy calls. She uses six moves to combine her two forces of 500,000 yellows, and with her remaining four moves, she crushes the invading blues. Grinning at Rinkus, she scoops all those blue forces off the board, then transfers the resources to her yellows. "So, I guess that leaves you with 4750,000 to protect your territory, and with limited resources, your position is useless. You may as well give up now."

Grabbing the dice and grumbling, Rinkus rolls. "Seven." With two moves, he plays the coveted Nuclear Wipe Out Card. "Drop the bomb to win, radioactive landmass, total destruction." Opening the drawer he sweeps a 750,000 being mass of yellows with resources off the board.

"How are you going to get out of yellow territory now? You've destroyed your path."

"I don't need to go home. My blues are taking over the entirety of ancient Earth."

"This game's no fun anymore," Syzygy says.

"You're a sore loser."

"I haven't lost…"

"Yeah, you have," Rinkus snickers. "Do you think there are any more mélange biscuits?

Syzygy whistles for Marcel.

They wait.

Nothing happens.

"He likes you better than me," Syzygy says.

Rinkus whistles.

Marcel whistles back, but doesn't fly up to the pavilion.

Impatient, Syzygy jumps up and runs downstairs.

Looking to the south, Rinkus admires the bougainvillea, breathes in the heady kalpolly, sips ambrosia, and wonders, for the kabillionth time, if Syzygy could be his paradise. He knows she could be, but there's that one thing missing, and a few bad qualities, but nothing's perfect. He sighs, his eyes drop, and that's when he sees the precious chronometer exposed from under the fuchsia and chartreuse paisley patterned velveteen cushion. Leaping up, surprisingly lightly for one so large, he tiptoes across the pavilion, repossesses the precious chronometer, and sets the cushion straight. Syzygy is devious. Rinkus wishes he weren't straightforward, and makes a resolution to not be.

The screen door slaps shut and Syzgy is running up the stairs.

Quickly, Rinkus walks out from underneath the canopy and goes to stand by the east edge. Surreptitiously he drops the precious chronometer into the hidden pocket of his aqua blue and silver arabesque kaftan.

Coming up behind him, Syzygy says, "Havila has invited you for supper."

He wants to ask what she's cooking because he's afraid it's cream of parsnip stew, and he wants to spend more time with Syzygy, but she stole his precious chronometer. Confused, all he can do is stare at her with his mouth open.

"Great," Syzygy blurts. "I'll tell her you're staying."

Flying up the stairs, Marcel swoops under the canopy and lands on Rinkus's shoulder. "I'll tell Havila you're not going." Then flies back downstairs.

"It's getting dark," Syzygy says with a shiver.

"Soon as the sun moves around the curve, it sure gets cold fast on Jikan," Rinkus says without looking at Syzygy.

Turning away, Syzygy starts untying the curtains on the pavilion.

Rinkus moves to help.

From downstairs, they hear the screen door slap then Havila coming up. On her golden tray are two carnelian mugs steaming with café latté. She doesn't say anything, merely sets one cup in front of Rinkus and the other in front of Syzygy.

Rinkus takes a sip. Quickly, he sets the carnelian cup back down.

Syzygy sips. "Havila, what kind of horrid sweetness is this?"

"How dare you talk to me like that," Havila hisses. With anger green on her face, she flings the golden tray so that it careens over the top of the new-fangled playing table, out the east side of the pavilion, high over the edge of the roof, and into the nearest orchard, where it lodges in a mélange tree. "Who do you think you are up here?"

Googly-eyed with surprise and shock, Rinkus and Syzygy sit as still as entranced hypnos.

"You're both self-willed godlets and your only concerns are greed and pleasure. I made that game of Resources for you to learn empathy and appreciation; to learn how not to hate."

Rinkus sputters, "Resources is just a game."

Eyes shooting lightning bolts, Havila contemplates this brazen ignorance. "Explain to me the difference between real and not real."

"Well…I mean," Rinkus sputters.

"We're real because we have consciousness, and we have emotions and bodies," Syzygy asserts.

"And in your magnificent consciousness you feel everything else?"

"No, of course not. . ." Syzygy begins to wither in embarrassment.

"So, what do you truly know?" Havila rages on, "I don't serve you because of what you believe you may or may not be. I serve you out of compassion."

Rinkus decides he'd better leave and starts to stand.

Havila turns on him, "Don't even think of running away. You are responsible."

Falling back into the overstuffed loveseat, Rinkus sputters, "Me? Responsible? For what?"

She looks at him as if he's as dumb as Einstein on Jupiter, "Everything."

"But . . . "

"He's merely my guest," Syzygy blurts. "Havila, what's got you all tormented?"

"Merely your guest?" Rinkus demands. "You make me sound as if I'm nothing more than a decagon."

"All this contrived hoopla about linear or circular time; how does it matter? Why would you live your life concerned with what you cannot control? That's as ignorant as it is egomaniacal," Havila glares. "Now quit playing around and get this game board converted back into a table before I throw out supper."

After they're done eating, Rinkus decides cream of parsnip stew is his new favorite.

Deep into the darkness, Havila sits awake in her haunt, alert, because who knows when the killer does not go into its lair?

When again Jikan comes back around into the light of the sun, Syzygy and Rinkus are entwined and sleeping on the new-fangled bed converted from the table.

Havila bangs loudly.

Glaring at Havila, Marcel says, "The whole world doesn't revolve around your schedule."

"But Jikan does." She opens the window above the kitchen sink. "Go and take a bird bath or something, and afterwards I want you to wake up the ignorants."

"Syzygy and Rinkus?"

"Who else would I be talking about?" Havila bangs her big ladle hard and loud on the onyx counter; waves her hand out the window.

Stamping his taloned foot, Marcel snaps, "You ought to learn to sleep; it's refreshing." When Havila's ladle comes careening his way, Marcel takes wing and arrows through the open window. "Maniac." Behind him he hears the window slam shut.

In the crisp and dewy morning, he flies toward the light. Free and high above the grouchiness of Havila and his responsibilities, Marcel gets lost in his own thoughts. Breathing in freshness, he soars and glides west over the beasties waking up for the day, some already drinking from the creek. Scattered between the edge of the field and the forest are the left over bones and guts that the killer didn't eat, and over which beetles, ricidues, and other scavengers and parasites are picking and fighting. Marcel arrows down, and picks up a nineteen-legged ricidue. Heavy with the weight he flaps a lumbered flap toward the villa.

When the ridicue manages to wiggle loose, it falls in a clump of hemsing bushes. Marcel arrows down to re-snatch it.

The howl wakes Syzygy and Rinkus.

"MMMMEEEEE, MMMMEEEE, MMEEEE MARCEL."

Crying, Rinkus throws the precious chronometer into the great rings of midnight blue and neon pink continuously vibrating and pulsing. "I want Marcel to come back," he sobs.

Disconsolate on the overstuffed loveseat, Syzygy sits with her legs pulled up, her arms wrapped around them and her head resting against her knees. "I don't know if I'm right anymore."

From the top of the stairs Havila announces, "I'm going after the killer."

Frozen in anxiety, standing on the edge of the roof, Syzygy and Rinkus watch Havila as she crosses the western field and disappears into the forest.

"YOOOUUUUU, YEAH, YOOOOUUUU."

"MMMMEEEEE, MMMMEEEE, MMEEEE."

The First of Many

By Allison Middlebrook

"Hey, Liz, come look at this."

I turned back from the mouth of the tunnel we'd just entered and swam up next to Chris. He was looking at someone else in the group, but expected me to see what he was holding in the darkness.

"Turn your lamp on it," I said, reaching out to touch his wrist. The echo of my voice in the radio was disorienting, and I had to concentrate in order to speak properly.

"Oh, sorry." He pointed his headlamp and the three of us crowded around him, looking down at what he'd found. It looked like a flat, polished stone.

"What is it?" Cassie asked, picking it up and turning it over. "It looks like some kind of rock. Ah, shit, I dropped it." We felt along the bottom of the cave and found it a moment later, holding it up in the light of our lamps.

"Is your camera working?"

"Yeah, it is. It looks like a tooth," Jake said. I held it out to him and he turned it over, pointing at the jagged edges sloping down from the tip. "Is it a shark tooth?"

"That'd have to be one huge shark. It's as big as your hand. It's gotta be a fossil or something," I said.

"Sharks haven't been in this area in hundreds of thousands of years," Cassie agreed. Being the compulsive researcher that she was, Cassie had looked up everything there was to read about these caves before we'd even booked the boat.

"How much do you think a museum would pay for something like this?" Chris asked, taking the tooth back.

"Not much," Jake said. "It probably washed in from the sea floor. These caves lead out into open waters, and anything that's spent that long down here is gonna be too eroded to be worth anything."

"Oh? And how do you know that, Mister Curator?" I teased. "Carbon dated any skeletons lately?"

"Come on," Cassie said. "We've only got a couple hours down here, and there are miles of tunnels to explore. Chris, you should keep that tooth. It'd make a nice paperweight or something."

"Yeah, you could be our own personal surfer-dude-turned-pencil-pusher," Jake laughed. "You can fight sharks in a business suit for a living."

"Uh-uh, don't even joke about sharks being down here," I said. "This is already creepy enough without the idea of something swimming around down here with us. Just pocket the tooth and let's get going. The sooner we get out of here, the happier I'll be."

"I'm pretty sure I just said there are no sharks in these waters, Liz," Cassie sighed. "And we're in the ocean, there's always something swimming around with us." Jake turned to look at me and shook his head. "You're the one who suggested this trip in the first place," he pointed out. "Now you wanna back out?"

"I suggested we go explore a reef or something," I argued, "not cave dive in the middle of a damned volcano."

"It's been extinct for almost a million years," Cassie said. "We'll be fine. Come on we're the first people to explore these caves. Aren't you excited? The only other thing that's been down here was some rich guy's souped-up robot-submarine. Let's go! I think the main cavern's up ahead."

We swam forward, falling into single file as the walls pressed in closer. I'd never been much of a fan of the dark, and the water in these caves was impenetrably black. I couldn't even see my hand in front of my face unless I looked directly at it with my headlamp. I couldn't hear much other than my own pulse and my friends' voices, and I focused on taking slow, deep breaths. Panicking here wouldn't do any good, and the others would make me go back and resurface alone if I freaked out. I paid for my part of this trip, I was damn well going to get my money's worth.

"This part of the cave gets pretty narrow," Chris said. We'd all studied the layout of the caves, but Chris had a better memory than any of us and had spent a few days with the maps we'd been given. "Let me go first and make sure we can fit through. If not, there's another way around that'll take us to the main cave."

After a bit of shuffling and a few muttered curses when someone's knee or elbow knocked into someone else's tender bits, Chris swam to the front of the line and continued forward. In the light of our combined lamps, we watched him kick toward a slight bend in the tunnel, following him as the rock narrowed until he had barely a hand's breadth between his tank and the wall.

"You gonna make it through?" I asked.

"Yeah, there's an overhang here that dips down a bit. I think I can get through if I take off my tank."

"Don't you dare," Cassie gasped. "What if you drop it?"

"I'm not gonna drop it, mom," he said. "Just stay back and don't go anywhere. I don't need you three getting lost in here."

"Wouldn't that be convenient?" I muttered.

"I heard that."

"You were supposed to."

We waited impatiently for Chris to unsnap the buckles that held his gear in place. He slipped the tank off, holding it close to his side as he shimmied through the narrow opening, and once he was through, he pulled it in behind him.

"Yeah, as long as you're careful, it should be easy enough," he said. "You guys can—"

Our radios crackled loudly, drowning out Chris's words, and we all flinched. There was a low rumbling sound, and a deafening crack that reverberated through the water, followed by a grinding sound that made my teeth chatter together.

I looked up at the ceiling of the tunnel and saw a crack that hadn't been there a minute ago running the width of where Chris had just squeezed through.

"Stay back!" I cried just as a shower of rubble and rocks the size of my head crashed down from the ceiling, knocking into each other and blocking our way.

"What the hell?" Jake demanded. He swam toward the collapse, but I grabbed his ankle and held him back.

"Don't go up to it, what if it shifts again and you get crushed?" I said.

"Chris!" Cassie called. "Chris, can you hear me? Are you okay? Oh God, guys, what if he's hurt? What are we going to do? He was going to lead us out of here!"

"We know these tunnels just as well as he does," Jake reassured her. "If push comes to shove, we'll find a way out. People know we're down here, they'll come looking for us before long."

"Not before we run out of air," I thought, but I kept that to myself. Aloud, I said, "Chris, can you hear us?"

We listened for a moment, and when nothing came over the radio, we moved a few feet closer to the rocks. The radio connection we were using didn't cover much area, and we didn't know how far Chris had gotten before the cave in.

"Chris!" Jake shouted.

"What?" came a disgruntled, tinny voice. It sounded like it was speaking from far away, but it was definitely Chris.

"Jesus Christ, man, we were scared you were dead," Jake sighed.

"Killed by a few rocks? I don't think so," he said. The connection crackled again, and his voice cut out. "—try to find a way around. Stay put…don't go anywhere."

"No," I said, "I don't think that's a good idea, Chris. If you go farther into the caves, you could get lost. We should try to find a way around to you, see if we can double back."

"Yeah," Cassie agreed, excited now by the idea of finding a way to solve the problem. "There are other ways into the main cave. If we backtrack, we can find a way to you through the main cave. Stay there and we'll come get you."

"Okay," Chris said, though his voice sounded less confident now. "Try to hurry, alright? I think I cut myself on one of the rocks."

"We'll be back," I promised as I moved past Jake and kicked off the side of the tunnel. "Come on, there was a branch off not too far back. I think it'll bring us around."

Together, we swam through the black water, searching the sides of the tunnel for an opening, anything that might lead us to Chris. I didn't like the idea of leaving him there alone in the dark. He was a smart guy, definitely braver than I was—if I was in his place, I'd be in hysterics. But the longer we took to find him, the more chance there was of him doing something dumb out of desperation.

"There," Jake said, pointing to my left. I turned to follow the light of his headlamp, but it suddenly wasn't there anymore. My heart leapt into my throat when I lost sight of him, and I reached back to grab his wrist.

"What the hell just happened?" I demanded.

"My light went out," he complained. "Christ, like everything else hasn't gone to crap already, now my light dies."

"Well did you charge it?" Cassie asked.

"Of course I charged it," Jake snapped. "I'm not an idiot. I charged it overnight. It should be full."

"Last night?" I said. "These things only have a six hour charge, it's already three o'clock! We were up at the crack of fucking dawn!"

"Well how the hell was I supposed to know they only hold a charge for six hours? Who buys headlamps that last that long when it takes hours to get to our diving point?"

"Guys," Cassie tried to say, but I cut her off.

"The person in charge of buying the lamps chooses which ones to get!" I snapped. "And guess who that was? You! Did you even read the label before you whipped your card out and walked out of the store?"

"No I didn't, because I didn't think anyone would be stupid enough to make diving gear that only holds a charge for six fucking hours!" he shouted. "You were supposed to tell me which brand to get, but you never texted me!"

"I called you! But do you ever answer your phone? No—"

"Guys!" Cassie shouted over us.

I looked away from Jake and bit my tongue.

"We're all worried and scared, and I'm pretty sure I speak for everyone when I say we want to get out of here as soon as we can," she said. "We can't do that if we wait around here arguing until we run out of air." She looked at her watch and then at the gauge that was attached to her harness. "We've got an hour and a half left before we need to be out of the tunnels and on our way back up. It's gonna take us at least half an hour to get to the surface, and we've got three hours of air left. That gives us an hour of wiggle room, and I'd rather that window not get any smaller. So can we kiss and make up for now? You can argue more once we're back on the boat."

I shot a glare at where I thought Jake's face was and dragged him up next to me. "I'm not kissing you," I said, "but Cassie's right. We need to get out of here fast. Hold onto me so you don't get lost or hit yourself on anything."

"Yes ma'am," Jake said dejectedly. He wound his arm between my tank and my lower back, making sure to give me room to move my legs.

The walls of the tunnel Jake had pointed out were wider than the last, but I didn't take comfort in that. If anything, not being able to feel the walls against my leg or my arm made me more nervous. We had a yard or two of visibility with our lights, and huddled together as we were, someone was going to be in the way of our line of sight.

"Liz, you take the lead," Cassie said suddenly.

"What? Why?" I demanded.

"Because I think we just found the main cave, and I don't like what I'm seeing."

"What are you seeing?" Jake asked as we emerged from the tunnel.

"Nothing."

If I'd thought the tunnels were dark, they were nothing compared to the cavern we'd just entered. Our lights pierced maybe two feet in front of us, and past the beams of yellow, the water was like ink.

"What the hell?" I whispered. "This isn't anything like what the reports said. Was it supposed to be this big?"

"I can't even see the bottom," Jake said.

I swam out in front of Cassie, making sure not to lose Jake in the process. The farther out we swam, the colder the water seemed to get, and by the time I lost my nerve, my fingers and toes were numb.

"We should go back to the wall, try to find a tunnel that leads to Chris. If we go out too far, we might not be able to find the same entrance again," I said. I didn't like the idea of being caught out in the middle of what could have been a vast space or a cave no wider than I was tall.

I looked out into the darkness and felt a cold shiver travel down my spine. I tried to tell myself that it was because of the sudden drop in temperature, but I knew that was a lie. Looking into that abyss was like standing on the edge of a cliff and hearing a little voice in the back of your head whisper, *Jump*.

"Come on," I said, feeling relieved when my voice didn't shake. "Let's hurry up and—Cassie! What the hell are you doing?"

Out of the corner of my eye, nearly too far away to see, Cassie's light turned to face us. She could have been anywhere between two and two hundred feet away, but what made my heart skip a beat was how dim her lamp was. Would it go out too?

"I…I don't know," Cassie replied, and her voice sounded far away, much like Chris's had behind the rocks. "I thought I saw something, and I was going to go look at it—"

"So you just go off on your own without saying a word?" Jake asked. He was justified in chastising her, but I couldn't help but feel a little annoyed with him. Hadn't I just gotten after him for not charging his lamp? Now he was trying to tell Cassie off? That just didn't sit right with me.

"Well I'm sorry," Cassie said, sounding exasperated and not at all apologetic, "but I really did see something. Come check it out with me. It was below us, but I don't think it's far away."

Despite every instinct in my body telling me not to do exactly what I was about to, I sighed and turned Jake and myself to face down, kicking hard to catch up. I made sure to stay close to the cavern wall so I would be able to tell up from down on the way back, and I tried to stretch my hand out to run along the stone and feel for anything that might serve as a landmark. God only knew how many tunnels there were in this volcano, and I didn't think I could stay calm if I lost the only bearings I had.

"There it is," Cassie said, and the sudden volume of her voice made me flinch in surprise. I'd gotten used to the silence of the water. "What is it?"

I followed the path of her lamp and swam closer to her, reaching out with my hands. It looked like an oblong rock that glowed faintly yellow. "Do you think there're algae down here? Plankton maybe? Something bioluminescent?"

"We're too far down for that," Cassie argued. "Plankton and algae can't survive this far under the surface. They need some kind of sunlight to photosynthesize."

"Then what the hell is it?"

"Uh guys," Jake said. He was uncharacteristically quiet, like he didn't want to voice what he had to say. "I don't think that's algae...look at the shape."

I swam forward a few more feet, but felt Jake resisting me. He didn't want to get closer any more than I did, but I needed to know what it was. I had a suspicion, and as much as I didn't want to be right, I had to know.

Cassie got to it first, and she picked it up in both hands. "Oh God," she whispered, "it's one of our headlamps." She held it up for me to see, and I took it from her, running my fingers over it. The cover was cracked and the strap was snapped, but it was unmistakable.

"I still have mine," Jake said. "It has to be Chris's. Do you think he made it out of the tunnel?"

"He could have. He knows this place better, he might have found a way—"

A blood-curdling scream cut me off, and I winced, trying to cover my ears for all the good it would do me. The sound was inside my facemask, I couldn't block it out.

"Cassie, what the hell!" Jake shouted. He must have tried to cover his ears too, because I couldn't feel his arm on my back anymore.

In the dim light, I could see the silhouette of Cassie's face; her eyes and mouth were stretched wide in terror. Tears streaked her cheeks and she pointed into the darkness. I turned and froze. It didn't make any sense. My brain didn't want to understand what my eyes were seeing; refused to process it. Jake's brain apparently worked better under pressure, though, because he kick-started mine by whispering in a trembling voice, "Oh my God…fuck, that's Chris!"

Just outside of the ring of light, half of a corpse rested on the sandy cavern floor. Well, it wasn't even half of a corpse.

Chris's head was still intact, his mask still in place with his hair floating in a halo around his face. His wetsuit was in tatters around what was left of his chest, and the scraps of tissue that hung from broken, exposed ribs cradled dark, silvery bits of…things.

I didn't want to know what they were.

Cassie screamed again, and I turned to look at her, wanting to rip the radio out of my ear.

"Cassie! Cassie, be quiet!" I hissed. She was having hysterics, sucking in huge gasps of air between sobs. I took Jake's arm and swam toward Cassie. When I reached her, I released Jake and held my hands up in front of her. "Cassie, look at me." She was panicking, trying to turn away from me. When she started screaming again, I grabbed her by her upper arms and gave her a hard shake. "Listen to me, dammit!"

Distantly, I heard Jake muttering, "No, no, God no, please no…fuck…," but I blocked out his voice, focusing on Cassie. I made eye contact with her and moved one of my hands to the side of her face.

"Cassie," I whispered, keeping my voice low so she had to really focus to hear me. "You need to calm down, alright? You're breathing too hard, too fast. You're going to run out of air."

Even as I spoke, I felt myself starting to panic too. I was in the dark, underwater, and one of my friends was dead. I should have been out of my mind with fear, but seeing Chris' mangled corpse slowed everything down, let me see the situation as if I was hovering just above my body instead of living this nightmare up close and personal.

"I know," Cassie gasped, closing her eyes as more tears slid down her cheeks. "But…but what killed—" She took a deep, shuddering breath and sobbed, "What killed him? We're supposed to be the only ones down here!"

I opened my mouth to answer and realized I didn't have an explanation, but was spared having to come up with something convincing by a sound that vibrated through the water. It wasn't quite a sound, more of a subsonic boom that rippled around us and rumbled in our chests. I didn't know what it was, but I knew I wanted at least a continent between myself and whatever had made it.

"Go. Go!" I said, pushing Cassie back toward the wall. Jake, who seemed to have frozen when the rumble sounded a second time, stared at me through wide eyes. I shoved him to the wall too and braced my fins against the cavern floor to shove him as far as I could. I was about to kick off when a thought occurred to me. His camera. It might have caught footage of whatever had murdered Chris. Then we could send someone down to kill whatever the hell it was so nothing like this ever happened again.

Twisting around, I swam toward the corpse of my friend, ignoring the reddish stain that tinged the water around it, refusing to see it as anything but a hunk of meat as I pulled the camera off the side of the facemask with trembling hands. I had just started to back away when I saw movement beyond the reach of my headlamp.

Every muscle in my body tensed, and I strained my eyes, trying to see past the black water, trying to listen past my own shaky breathing, failing to calm my thundering heart and shove it back down out of my throat.

Silent as a ghost, a form slid just close enough to show bumpy, pale, scaled skin like some crossbreed of a crocodile and a snake, and I saw an enormous, long, talon-tipped leg as thick around as my thigh scraped along the bottom of the cavern. Hot tears stung my eyes as I followed its movement, watching it come closer to me with every lazy step that dragged it along the stone like a fat-bellied barge. The rumbling sounded again, and I could tell that it was coming from this…this thing, whatever it was. Its head came into the light, and I saw enormous, bloody teeth lining a stunted snout and small, cloudy eyes no larger than my fist.

The creature's jaws parted, and it rumbled again, nudging Chris's body with its snout. It rested its teeth almost gingerly over his shoulder and dragged him off into the darkness.

My heart didn't kick back into gear until the rumbling stopped, and with it, all of my other senses came back online at once. I tasted my tears, felt fear-sweat slicking my skin beneath my wet suit, and lastly I heard my friends shouting my name, trying desperately to make me answer.

"Elizabeth!" Cassie screamed. "Elizabeth, what the hell was that thing!"

I shook myself and tucked Chris' camera into a pouch on my gear, pumping my legs hard to rejoin Jake and Cassie. "I don't know what it was," I said steadily, even as my stomach twisted, threatening to make me sick. "We need to get out of here. Now."

"No shit," Jake said.

"You don't have to be nasty," Cassie snapped. "Elizabeth's just trying to—"

"Cassie!" I cried as the pale, tooth-filled maw of the creature opened behind her and closed around her chest. Jake screamed. I screamed. Cassie stared at us in horror and confusion as she was yanked back into the darkness.

"Fuck!" Jake wailed, and he lashed out in the water. His fin caught me on the side of my head, knocking my facemask loose. I slapped my hands against it before too much water got in, and I spluttered, swearing as I kicked off the ground.

"Jake!" I called. "Jake, you're going the wrong way! You missed the tunnel!" I watched him kick desperately toward the wall, watched his arms wave about as his hands skimmed the stone, but I was too far away for my light to do him any good. He'd gotten too much of a head start, and I couldn't catch up. My radio must have been damaged by the water, because I couldn't hear him breathing, couldn't hear him crying or cursing or shouting.

Suddenly, his kicking became more erratic, his motions more jerky, and he veered sharply to the left. I followed him, swimming as fast as I could, hauling myself along the wall and using any purchase I could find to gain on him. Then, he suddenly disappeared right into the face of the rock. I caught the edge of his fin as he slipped into a fissure that was just wide enough for us to fit through. He tried to kick me, but I grabbed his ankle and made eye contact with him, shaking my head slowly. I pulled myself into the space, but it was too cramped. Jake had to move up and back some to let me in, and it put him closer to the opening. He didn't like that, and tried to tell me so, but I pointed at my ear, shaking my head again to tell him I couldn't hear him. I didn't need to hear his words to understand what he wanted to say.

He was scared, desperate, and he knew we were going to die. I felt the exact same way, knew the same things, and the only way I could comfort him was to reach out and take his hand.

"I'm scared," he said, and I read the words on his lips.
I nodded and squeezed his fingers tightly. "I am too."

In the silence, we held each other's gazes and listened for the monster, waited to feel the rumble in our chests. How far away was it? Could it get to us here? It was too big to fit its head through the fissure, but how well could it use those talons? It could scoop us out like grubworms and we wouldn't be able to do anything about it.

The rumbling returned, and I felt Jake's fingers tighten around mine. He was crying, his eyes staring off into the distance as the creature's call filled our hiding place and vibrated in our very bones.

I flinched when I heard a sound like metal scraping wood, and I looked past Jake's shoulder to see a curved claw as long as my forearm resting just inside of the fissure. It didn't try to move farther in, didn't try to grab Jake's leg, which was barely a yard away. It just rested there, waiting. Jake's eyes widened and his mouth pulled back into something that looked like a pained smile, but I knew he was trying not to scream. I'm sure my face was doing something similar.

"Don't move," I whispered.

Maybe he couldn't read lips as well as me, or maybe he was just too scared to listen to reason, but he turned his head to look over his shoulder and his entire body jerked. He twisted around, inadvertently driving his elbow into my stomach and forcing the air from my lungs. I gasped for breath as he lashed out with his feet, trying to kick the claw away.

It struck with unbelievable speed.

I didn't even see it move, not a twitch or even the thought of moving. One minute it was there, the next Jake's leg was hanging from a couple of ligaments and sinews attached to his knee.

I didn't need a radio to hear Jake's screams of pain, and he twisted around to face me again. His face was pale, his mouth and eyes impossibly wide as he clawed at me, trying to get away, deeper into the fissure. But there was nowhere else to go. He'd pushed me as far into our hiding spot as I could fit. Still he pushed me, either trying to get me farther away from the thing or just get me out of the way. I wanted to believe he was trying to save me, but the crazed look in his eye suggested otherwise.

Jake's struggling grew weaker as shock settled in, and he stopped trying to crush me against the rocks. He was pale and sweating, and even in the dim light my dying headlamp provided, I saw him smile weakly at me.

"Go."

He reached out, pressed his hands against either side of the fissure and propelled himself backward. He ripped his mask off, grabbed the creature's talon and sank his teeth into its scaly hide. It didn't react in the slightest. Jake held on tight as the thing ripped him out of the fissure, and I took that as my cue to leave. I shoved off of the rock...

...and went nowhere.

I pushed forward, struggling to gain a foothold on the smooth stone around me, and I heard metal scrape against the rock. My tank was stuck! I swore viciously and unclipped the buckles that held my gear in place. I started panicking, felt the adrenaline pumping through my veins, felt my limbs shaking with unspent energy, and gasped at huge lung-fulls of air. And just before I lost my nerve, I grabbed my survival knife, ripped off my mask and hurled myself at the opening.

I burst into the darkness of the cavern and clawed my way toward the tunnel we'd lost Chris in. I knew my chances of getting out of there alive. I was a recreational diver, not a professional. I couldn't hold my breath for ten minutes; I couldn't even do it for three. And even if I made it to the surface, the bends would kill me before I ever reached the boat.

But I'd be damned if I let some scaly-assed, slithery, crocodile wannabe that probably crawled out of Australia's asshole eat me.

I scrabbled along the wall, feeling the weight of the water press in on me as I pawed around like a blind puppy. My lungs burned, and I fought my body not to expel the spent air, to hold on for just another minute. Another thirty seconds, that was all I needed, and I would find the tunnel. I would feel the lip under my fingers and pull myself into it. My headlamp wasn't dead yet; I could still see enough through the saltwater that stung my eyes to know I was going in what I hoped was the right direction.

I didn't get my thirty seconds. I didn't even get five. Something pinched my upper thigh, and I coughed out my air, gagging on the water I couldn't keep from inhaling. I reached down to find what was on my leg and felt bumpy skin under my fingertips. I waited for the pain to register, but my brain seemed too preoccupied with trying to figure out why my lungs weren't working anymore.

In my last moments, just before I lost everything, I reached out, feeling along the monster's head until I found its brow. I hooked my fingers under its eyelid and drove the knife into its eye. The blade sank to the hilt and the beast released me with a pained shriek.

I floated in the water, unable to move, unable to breathe, and I watched the light of my headlamp finally fade away, leaving me and my friends to the darkness in the cavern.

Author Contact Info and Bio:

Jason Peters – Editor – JasonAberrant@yahoo.com

 Jason Peters is a Screenwriter, Author, and Founder/Editor-In-Chief of Aberrant Literature. Residing in Los Angeles, his works include the horror/comedy/crime-thriller screenplay *Obsidian*, and the short story *A Trial By Any Other Name*. He is actively writing his first novel, to be released in 2016. Please contact via e-mail to discuss business opportunities, and follow on Twitter @AberrantLit.

Ben Nardolilli – Author – Bnardolilli@gmail.com

 Ben Nardolilli currently lives in New York City. His work has appeared in Perigee Magazine, Red Fez, Danse Macabre, The 22 Magazine, Quail Bell Magazine, Elimae, fwriction, THEMA, Pear Noir, The Minetta Review, and Yes Poetry. He blogs at mirrorsponge.blogspot.com and is actively working towards publication of his first novel.

Author Contact Info and Bio (cont.):

Tracy Sherwood – Author – TSWrite8@aol.com

Tracy Sherwood is a Pushcart Award nominated writer and prize-winning screenwriter, as well as the author of the recently released contemporary drama novel, Death Grip.

Rex Brooke – Author – RHBrooke@gmail.com

A graduate in Literature from UCSD, Rex Brooke, self-appointed "master of none," has been a lifeguard, farm hand, bartender, secretary, carpenter, and teacher. He recently returned to the small town in which he was raised in order to take care of his blind, 96 year old mother, and perhaps, to know the place for the first time.

Joan Brown – Author – JoanBrown51@yahoo.com

Joan Brown is a freelance writer in Portland, Oregon. She believes in thinking critically and speaking-out. What she mostly writes about is the human condition; how the quality of our lives is influenced by social, political and economic concerns, and how we in turn create our culture. To learn more about Brown, please visit her website: https://sites.google.com/a/pdx.edu/joan-a-brown/home

Author Contact Info and Bio (cont.):

Allison Middlebrook – Author -
AMiddlebrook96@gmail.com

      Allison Middlebrook is the author of many works such as *Getting Away with It* and *Behind Closed Doors*, and has been writing since she was old enough to hold a pencil. She aspires to one day escape the confines of her Washington home full of crazy relatives and pets into the fantastical worlds about which she writes.

Jared Wojcik - Graphic Design - Jared.wojcik@gmail.com
      Jared is a freelance Graphic Designer based out of Los Angeles, CA. He designed and created the Aberrant Literature logo, in addition to numerous other logos and design elements for prominent businesses, including Fortune 1000 companies. Please contact via e-mail to discuss design-related business opportunities.

There's plenty more Aberrant Literature for you to experience...

Visit our blog for new and exclusive stories and articles at www.AberrantLiterature.com

Stay in touch with Aberrant Literature via:

Facebook: Aberrant Literature

Twitter: @AberrantLit

If you liked this Aberrant Literature Short Fiction Collection, please post a review at Amazon, and let your friends know about us. All honest and unbiased reviews are appreciated.

Stay tuned for more collections to come!